THE GILDED CAGE

The third in a saga about the Yorks, Lancasters and

Nevilles,

whose family feud started the "Cousin's War",

now known as the Wars of the Roses,

told by Cecily "Cecylee" Neville (1415-1495),

the Thwarted Queen

Cynthia Sally Haggard

Spun Stories Press
Washington DC 20036

Published by Spun Stories Press

Designed by Cynthia Sally Haggard

Manufactured in the United States of America

ISBN: 0984816925
ISBN-13: 978-0-9848169-2-7

For my dear friend Beth Gessert Franks
for all her endurance of Cecylee

Contents

Acknowledgments

This book took me seven years to write. I could not have done it without the help of many people. The first person who deserves thanks is my friend Beth Franks, a talented writer in her own right, who patiently went through several drafts of *Thwarted Queen*, and made innumerable suggestions for improvement.

Next, I want to thank my wonderful editor Catherine Adams, formerly of the *Iowa Book Doctors* now of *Inkslinger Editing*, for her structural editing of the manuscript early on, and the many helpful suggestions she made then that brought the novel to a new level. This summer, Catherine did a magnificent job in the line-by-line content and copyediting, gently pruning the manuscript to give it what I hope is a polished, professional feel. Any mistakes are my own!

I also wish to thank Lord Barnard of Raby Castle in County Durham for his interest in my novel, and for allowing Clifton Sutcliffe, the docent, to take me on a personal tour of Cecily's childhood home in July 2007. Mr. Sutcliffe showed me the Keep where Cecylee was locked up by her father, and explained to me about the wooden walkways that criss-crossed Castle Raby to make passage from one tower to another easy in the event of a raid. I am also indebted to him for bringing to my attention John Wolstenholme Cobb's *History and Antiquities of Berkhamsted*, in which he quotes *The Orders and Rules of the Princess Cecill*.

I wish to thank the United States Military Academy Department of History for allowing me to use the map of England and France circa 1422, and for Emerson Kent in helping me to find it.

I was privileged to take classes with many wonderful teachers during my long journey with *TQ*. I wish to thank Mark Spencer, professor of English and Dean of the School of Arts and Humanities at the University of Arkansas at Monticello for his class *Successful Self-Publishing*, given during the spring of 2011; Curtis Sittenfeld, author of *American*

Wife, for her sensitive reading of the novel during the *2010 Napa Valley Writer's Workshop*; Amy Rennert of the Amy Rennert Agency for her class *Secrets of Publishing Success* given at Book Passage in Corte Madera CA, during the fall of 2006; Janis Cooke-Newman, author of *Mary: Mrs. A. Lincoln*, for her invaluable help on the end of the novel; Michael Neff, creator of *Web del Sol*, for his wonderful classes on craft at the *2005 Harper's Ferry Workshop*; Junse Kim, who taught *Introduction to Fiction: You Can't Build a House without Foundations* and Otis Haschemeyer, who taught *Introduction to the Novel* at the *Writing Salon* in Bernal Heights San Francisco during the fall of 2004. I could not have written and published my novel without the help of these professionals.

My friend Beth Robertson deserves thanks for sharing her expertise on Chaucer, and her knowledge of subversive activity amongst medieval ladies, who would often read material that would not have pleased their husbands. Such inflammatory scrolls were secreted in the saddle bags of Abbesses and other ladies, who were ostensibly just making a social call.

I wish to thank the following writers for reading the manuscript and making useful suggestions: Kristin Abkemeyer, Myrna Loy Ashby, Sharyn Bowman, Peter Brown, Julie Corwin, Eric Goldman, Joy Jones, Phil Kurata, Nadine Leavitt-Siak, Michelle McGurk, Amanda Miller, Rose Murphy, Nicole Nelson, Dan Newman, Desirée Parker, Walter Simson, Kevin Singer, Judy Wertheimer, Jun Yan.

Last but not least, I wish to thank the talented Heather Hayes for donating her time to model for Cecylee; her friend, Whitney Arostegui, for donating her time to shoot the photos that were used for the cover of the novel; Dave Graham for donating his time to convert my cover images to CMYK mode and teaching me to make the necessary edits; my husband Georges Rey for prodding me to continue with Cecylee, and my sister Melanie, for giving me the idea in the first place.

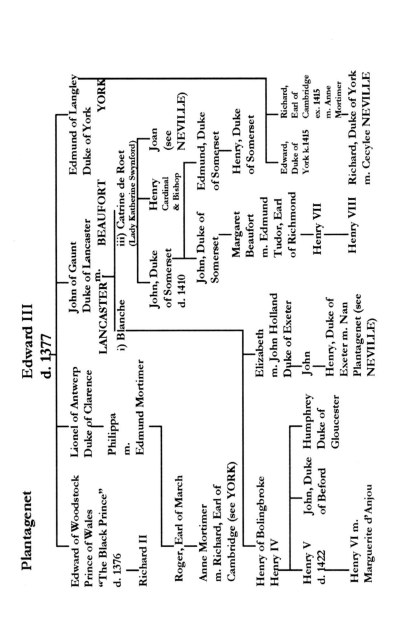

Plantagenet

Edward III
d. 1377

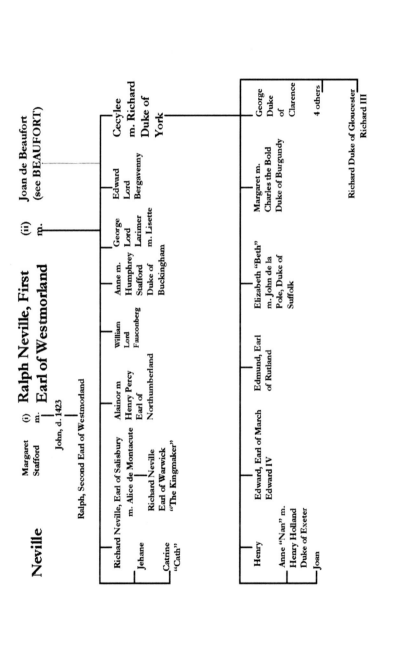

Neville

Margaret Stafford (i) m. **Ralph Neville, First Earl of Westmorland** (ii) m. Joan de Beaufort (see BEAUFORT)

John, d. 1423

Ralph, Second Earl of Westmorland

First marriage (i):
- Richard Neville, Earl of Salisbury m. Alice de Montacute
  - Jehane
  - Catrine "Cath"
  - Richard Neville Earl of Warwick "The Kingmaker"
- Alainor m Henry Percy Earl of Northumberland

Second marriage (ii):
- William Lord Fauconberg
- Anne m. Humphrey Stafford Duke of Buckingham
- George Lord Latimer m. Lisette
- Edward Lord Bergavenny
- Cecylee m. Richard Duke of York
  - Henry
  - Anne "Nan" m. Henry Holland Duke of Exeter
  - Joan
  - Edward, Earl of March Edward IV
  - Edmund, Earl of Rutland
  - Elizabeth "Beth" m. John de la Pole, Duke of Suffolk
  - Margaret m. Charles the Bold Duke of Burgundy
  - George Duke of Clarence
  - 4 others
  - Richard Duke of Gloucester Richard III

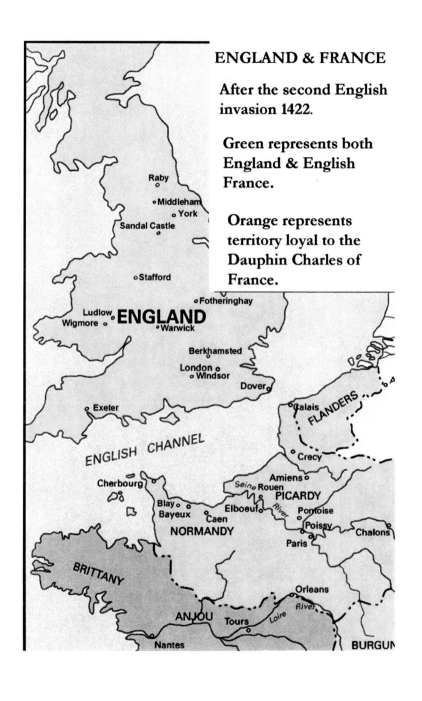

ENGLAND & FRANCE

After the second English invasion 1422.

Green represents both England & English France.

Orange represents territory loyal to the Dauphin Charles of France.

BOOK III
🍀 🍀 🍀 🍀 🍀

When she is fully readye she hath a lowe masse in her chamber,
and after masse she taketh something to recreate nature;
and soe goeth to the chappell hearinge the devine service, and two lowe
masses;
from thence to dynner,
during the tyme whereof she hath a lecture of holy matter...
After dinner she giveth audyence to all such as hath any matter to shewe
unto her by the space of one hower;

FROM ORDERS AND RULES OF THE PRINCESS
CECILL
QUOTED BY JOHN WOLSTENHOLME COBB (1883)
HISTORY & ANTIQUITIES OF BERKHAMSTED

Chapter 1
Abbey of Beaumont-lès-Tours, Tours, France
Spring 1444

"Enchanted," murmured William de la Pole, fourth Earl of Suffolk, as he stooped to kiss the outstretched hand of Marguerite d'Anjou. A vibrant young lady, her full lips parted as she smiled, revealing perfect white teeth. The King of England had already fallen in love with a secretly obtained portrait of her, but in the flesh, this visage was intoxicating. Her black hair had been braided into plaits and wound around her head, and her eyes glowed like a stoked fire, enormous and black. Marguerite d'Anjou was but fifteen years old.

Suffolk had come to France at the urging of his young master, the King of England, who had made him promise to obtain the lady for him. His patron, Cardinal Beaufort, had told him that the marriage would form the centerpiece of the peace negotiations labored on for the past two years. It was now Suffolk's duty to interview the lady herself and ascertain if she were truly fit to be England's queen. He offered his arm. "What do you know of England?"

"There has been a war between the English and the French for the past one hundred years," replied Marguerite. "So far, no one has won this fight. Though the English gained a great victory at Agincourt thirty years ago when King Henry's father was king, they have not been able to press their claims to the throne of France. If I were King of England, I would sue for peace."

"So you would never make war?"

"I did not say that. If an enemy dared to attack me, I would mount my best horse and lead the charge."

"Marguerite!" exclaimed her mother Ysabeau, the Duchess of Lorraine, who walked a few paces behind. But Suffolk laughed, delighted.

"But you need men to fight for you," observed Suffolk, patting her arm. "How would you persuade them?"

"A queen must be many things," said Marguerite. "She must be a good wife to her lord and provide him with heirs. She must be a gracious hostess to everyone at court. She must find suitable husbands for the young women under her patronage. She must be charitable to those in need. She must encourage education and art. But, above all, she must inspire her people." She turned her dark gaze up to Suffolk's face. "I say to you, sir, that if such a queen requested her people to fight for her, do you not think they would follow?"

Suffolk chuckled as he kissed her hand with a flourish. This young lady had just given a perfect description. "Tell me," he murmured, "do you seek to emulate anyone in particular?"

"My lord father," replied Marguerite without pause.

Suffolk glanced around, but her father was standing some feet away, engaged in animated conversation with his steward. He narrowed his eyes. Did she really mean that? Réné of Anjou, King of Naples and Sicily, was described as a man of many crowns and no kingdoms. He had been struggling to take control of his vast inheritance without great success, even being taken prisoner by Philip III, Duke of Burgundy.

"And my lady mother," remarked Marguerite.

That was more like it, thought Suffolk, smiling at her eager face. Duchess Ysabeau had raised an army to rescue her husband from captivity.

"And my lady grandmother," said Marguerite.

"The Duchess of Aragon?"

Marguerite smiled, showing off her perfect teeth.

Suffolk whistled under his breath as he stroked his beard. Yolande of Aragon had dominated French politics until her death two years ago. Suffolk had heard rumors that it was Duchess Yolande who orchestrated the appearance of Joan of Arc to inspire the French troops. If Marguerite were anything like her grandmother, she would be a formidable lady indeed. But perhaps she was exactly what the young king needed, for it was plain that he was weak and easily led by his councilors. The king's council was barely able to govern these days on account of the continuing feud between Humphrey Plantagenet, Duke of Gloucester, and Cardinal Beaufort. Suffolk considered. Should he be concerned about promoting such a charismatic young lady to be Queen of England? What of his own position? He was entirely dependent on the king's favor. He glanced over at her as she moved into the Abbot's parlor.

"My daughter likes also to dance," murmured her father, standing at his elbow. He signaled to a servant to pour wine. "My daughter requests that she dance the Tarantella for you."

Suffolk inclined his head.

Marguerite began the dance by curtseying low, first to Suffolk, and then to each of her parents. She danced lightly, moving through the supple rhythms with ease and grace, her steps matching the rhythms exactly, her bearing and gestures adding beauty to the music.

Suffolk watched for a few minutes. The young lady was beautiful, personable, articulate and displayed impeccable carriage. She smiled at him as she danced, and he could not help smiling back. He did not fear her, for he and Marguerite were going to be the greatest of friends. He turned to René. "Your Grace, you have a lovely daughter. She has all the qualities one would hope for in a queen. I would now like to make a formal request for the hand of your daughter Marguerite."

"By all means," agreed René. "My daughter is a jewel, as you can see. Her mother and I are happy that you think her worthy to be Queen of England. But there is one matter I should warn you about. It shames me to say this, but I have no money, so I will be unable to provide my daughter with a dowry."

"No dowry?" exclaimed Suffolk.

Duchess Ysabeau raised her head, and Marguerite paused for a measure while she shot a sharp look in Suffolk's direction. Then she began to dance once more.

Réné lowered his voice. "I inherited the Duchy of Anjou ten years ago, but I get no revenues from it because it is owned by your king. I tried to claim the Kingdom of Naples, but was forced to cede it to my cousin Alfonso of Aragon. My friend, I am poor and cannot provide for my daughter as I would wish."

"But you surely don't mean to send your daughter to England with nothing."

"I would be better able to provide for her, *mon ami*, if I had my lands back. I demand that King Henry give me the counties of Maine and Anjou as part of the marriage settlement."

Suffolk choked on his wine. "But the English people will never agree," he said between coughs. "If you insist on this, Your Grace, you will make your daughter unpopular. The English will resent her for the terms of this treaty. Is that how you wish her to begin as Queen of England?"

Réné made a dismissive gesture. "I don't see that the opinion of peasants should have any bearing on matters of state. The King of England will protect Marguerite from all that."

"England is not like France, my friend. People are in the habit of expressing their opinions much more freely. Being unpopular with the people could be costly. The King of England has to please the London merchants, otherwise they will not give him loans."

Réné shrugged. "Those are my terms. Charles, Count of Nevers, wants my daughter also, so I suggest you hurry."

Suffolk glanced at Marguerite again. She was perfect, and the King of England was already in love with her; he would never forgive Suffolk if Marguerite didn't become his bride.

Chapter 2
Pontoise, English France
Saint Joseph's Eve
March 18, 1445

Cecylee shivered, the piercing air of March sending threads of freezing air through the thick fur mantle. She stood a little way back from the riverbank, careful not to get too close to the soft mud oozing up between the reeds and river grasses and threatening to soil her slippers. This Saint Joseph's Eve, she stood by the banks of the Seine, waiting for the queen's entry into Pontoise.

Cecylee measured time by how long it had been since Joan's passing. Before, everything seemed filled with sunlight. Now, the clouds had rolled in. How long would it be before she could join her daughter? It had already been three years.

Richard had agreed to name Blaybourne's son Edward and christened him in a small private ceremony in the chapel of Saint Romain where Joan was buried. One month after Edward's first birthday, Cecylee bore a son that Richard named Edmund, after his uncle Edmund Mortimer. Richard was ecstatic about this son's birth and a magnificent ceremony for his christening was held in Rouen Cathedral with a large number of dignitaries present. As a mark of special favor, the cathedral chapter allowed Richard to use Duke Rollo's font for Edmund's christening. Much was made of this honor, for this was the font at which Duke Rollo of Normandy, an ancestor of William the Conqueror, had been baptized into Christianity in the year 912. It had been kept covered and unused for over five hundred years.

Eleven months after Edmund's birth, Cecylee gave Richard a daughter named Beth.

Cecylee had mixed feelings about bearing so many children in such a short span of time: Joan, Nan, Henry, Edward, Edmund, Beth. She was in her prime, yet the fear of death was a continual presence. Now she stood with Richard, holding Nan's hand as she peered through the murky gloom for the barge that bore the new Queen of England from Paris. Sixteen-year-old Marguerite d'Anjou had been married by proxy to twenty-three-year-old King Henry of England a couple of weeks back and now began her journey to England.

Cecylee had heard much of the new queen. She'd heard that Marguerite d'Anjou had won golden opinions at the French court where she'd been living for the past year with her aunt Queen Marie d'Anjou of France. Charles of Valois, Duke of Orléans, was reported to have said that this woman "excelled all others, as well in beauty as in wit, and was of stomach and courage more like to a man that to a woman."

"Are they here, Mama?"

"Not yet, my sweet. Are you sure you're warm enough?"

"I am perfectly comfortable," replied five-year-old Nan gravely, her blue-grey eyes bearing Richard's expression. "Chatelaine keeps me warm."

Cecylee smiled, adjusting the child's soft fur hood. Nan was inseparable from her kitten. The tiny grey animal had hooked its claws into the thick sable, so that it reclined on Nan's shoulder. "She's not too heavy for you?"

"Not yet," replied Nan.

"You shouldn't have allowed her to bring that cat," muttered Richard.

"She adores Chatelaine," whispered Cecylee. "Besides," she added, tilting her head as a sudden thought struck her, "it looks like a fur collar, don't you think?"

Richard's smile eased away the lines of his face.

"Why don't you take her for a walk?" murmured Cecylee, thinking it would be well for Richard to spend time with his daughter.

She clasped her hands together for warmth beneath her furs as they left. Now that Marguerite d'Anjou was Queen of England, she was no longer first lady of the land. She would have to yield precedence to a girl fourteen years younger, and of an age to be her own child. If Marguerite bore the king sons, Richard would cease to have any claim on the English throne. Perhaps it would be best if she and Richard went back to their estates in England, even to Richard's favorite residence at Fotheringhay, and lived out their lives in peace. As it was, Richard did not have many friends amongst the councilors who surrounded the king. They were divided into two camps. The Duke of Gloucester, supported by Richard, argued vociferously for the continuance of the war in France; Cardinal Beaufort and his allies Suffolk and Somerset favored peace. The king was entirely dominated by Beaufort, Suffolk, and their cronies, who would stop at nothing to get their way, including accusing Gloucester's wife of witchcraft.

She crossed herself and shivered. At least they'd got rid of York by posting him abroad.

"Well met, my lady York," said a soft voice.

Cecylee turned to see Jacquetta de St. Pol, Duchess of Bedford, smiling. The Duchess was a lady of her age, elegantly dressed in grey furs that set off her grey eyes and pale complexion. She had caused a scandal some ten years before, when, as recent widow to the powerful Duke of Bedford and aunt-by-marriage to the king, she had married Sir Richard Woodville, a mere knight. Cecylee had admired Jacquetta for the courage she'd shown in braving the wrath of the King of England to marry this man who had been but a chamberlain to the Duke of Bedford.

"May I introduce my husband Sir Richard Woodville?"

A man with a well-cut profile came forward and bowed low. Cecylee felt a twinge as she stared at this handsome face now emerging from a bow.

He looked down and smiled. "My lady York: The pleasure is all mine."

Cecylee's cheeks burned as she compared him with Blaybourne. Everyone sneered at Sir Richard's low birth, and yet his manners were courtly, his bearing elegant. The conundrum of Blaybourne reappeared: How could a mere peasant have the manners of an aristocrat? Didn't blood run true? How could this be possible unless he had some blue blood in his veins?

"Handsome, isn't he?" murmured Jacquetta.

Cecylee started and blushed as she realized she must have been staring at Sir Richard, almost as if she were trying to make out his shape from beneath the folds of the lavish cloak he'd wrapped himself in.

Jacquetta chuckled deep in her throat.

Cecylee stiffened.

"This is our eldest child," said Jacquetta nudging a diminutive form towards her. "Make your curtsey, *chérie*."

A tiny figure swathed in a green velvet cloak swept a deep curtsey. As she bent her head, a lock of hair spilled from her hood. The color was golden, vibrating with light.

"This is my Élisabeth."

Cecylee looked down into a pair of brown eyes. How strange. For wasn't brown a warm color? This child's eyes were cold, the color of stream-washed stones.

"How old is she?"

"Nigh on eight," replied Jacquetta.

Jacquetta was her age. She had a beautiful daughter Joan's age, and she had married for love. Cecylee might outrank Jacquetta among the ladies of court, but God was punishing her.

"Mama?" Cecylee turned and saw that Nan and Richard had returned. She made the introductions.

"I don't like Élisabeth," whispered Nan as Richard made conversation with the Woodvilles. "She stares at you in a mean way."

"Hush, my sweet," replied Cecylee, looking around to see if anyone had heard her. "Ladies do not pass remarks about people in public."

A slap of water made her turn. From the direction of Paris, a dark shape emerged silently through the mists. Several swathed figures sat in it, but the only color that emerged from the deep gloom was a faint gleam of gold shining dully from the head of one of the figures. Propelled by the rhythmical rising and falling of the oars, the barge drew closer and fanfare shattered the quiet. Richard took her hand, and they moved across the thick carpets that had been placed at shore's edge as the crowned figure arose and stepped lightly to land.

"By the Grace of God, Marguerite, Queen of England and France, and Lady of Ireland!" the herald roared.

Suffolk disembarked next and knelt. "My dear lady," he said in his mellifluous voice, "May God bless you and keep you. This day is a blessing, for England gains a great queen."

A chill wind blew as Marguerite hastened forward to help him up. "Rise, *mon cher ami.*" she said. "I am most grateful for all that you have done for me. You have my most especial favor."

Suffolk patted her hand and smiled as Richard thinned his lips.

Chapter 3
Pontoise, English France

When Marguerite d'Anjou first met the English Court at Pontoise on Saint Joseph's Eve in March 1445, the Duke of York was the first to kiss her hand. Marguerite was struck by the somber coloring of his raiment and the serious expression on his face. But as she motioned him to rise, a smile lit his face, warming those blue-grey eyes. Just behind Duke Richard was his wife, who sank into a deep and graceful curtsey with her head bent. Duchess Cecylee was very pretty in an English sort of way, with grey eyes, a lily-white complexion and fair hair that had been braided up into an elaborate hairstyle. She wore a grey gown of fine wool, further setting off those eyes. For a woman who had already borne her lord six children, the Duchess was enviably slender. It was obvious her lord adored her, for he could scarce keep his eyes away.

As the duchess rose from her curtsey, she smiled, making her grey eyes sparkle. "Welcome to England, my dear," she said in that ugly, clattering Norman French with its rounded vowels, sharp consonants, and frequent heavy stresses.

Marguerite flinched. She would have to accustom herself to the elegant and beautiful French language being mangled in such a fashion.

"My lord Duke and I hope you will be happy in England," continued the duchess. "We will try to make it so."

As she spoke, Duchess Cecylee took in Queen Marguerite's appearance. But she lowered her lashes, and said nothing.

Marguerite lifted her chin. How dare the duchess criticize her.

York cleared his throat. "We are blessed indeed with the arrival of this most beauteous princess from France." He murmured various other compliments, but Marguerite was distracted by Duchess Cecylee, who beckoned to a young boy to come forward. He held various packages done up in twine.

"I have this day been to the merchants of Pontoise," she remarked.

York raised an eyebrow as he turned to his wife.

She put a hand on his arm. "Dickon," she said, "you know we women must look our best for the state banquet we are to give our queen tonight." She turned to Marguerite. "May I present to you my maid Jenet?"

A slender brown maid curtseyed low.

"Jeanette is from Picardy," continued the Duchess in her heavy Norman-French accent, "but has lived many years in England and knows English fashions. If it pleases you, I would like to invite you to my apartments after Mass to see what I have bought."

Marguerite's cheeks warmed. Had they heard she'd been so short of money she'd been obliged to pawn her silver plate to the kind-hearted Countess of Somerset so that she could pay the wages of her sailors? Marguerite involuntarily glanced at her new friend Eleanor Beauchamp, Countess of Somerset, who stood by her side.

Marguerite turned back to Duchess Cecylee. "I thank you, madam, for your most kind attentions, but I have brought with me five barons and baronesses, seventeen knights, sixty-five squires and sundry others. King Henri has been kind enough to provide me with the services of the Countesses of Suffolk and Somerset. Therefore I can manage, I assure you."

Duchess Cecylee compressed her lips, a perfect rose-pink filling her lily-white complexion. An elegant lady in sky-blue satin took this opportunity to move forward. She dropped an exquisite curtsey. "My lady Queen, I am Jacquetta de Saint Pol, Duchess of Bedford, and sister to Isabelle of Luxembourg, Countess de Guise."

Marguerite smiled into the lovely face of this stranger who pronounced French so beautifully. Isabelle de Guise was married to her father's brother Charles, the Count of Maine.

"How is dearest Isabelle?" continued Jacquetta, as Marguerite motioned her to rise. "Has she had her child?"

"*Tante* Isabelle is very well and sends to you her love," replied Marguerite, delighted to meet the countrywoman she'd heard much about. "She was brought to bed of a beautiful daughter called Louise." Marguerite motioned Jacquetta to a seat: "What can you tell me of England?"

"Many things, *chérie*, but all in good time. May I present to you my husband Sir Richard Woodville?"

Sir Richard came forward, bowed low, knelt, and kissed the Queen's hand. "*Enchanté*," he murmured, smiling up at her.

"And here is little Élisabeth, my eldest," continued Jacquetta as a diminutive figure curtseyed low.

"*Ma petite*," exclaimed Marguerite, raising the child from her curtsey. She planted kisses on each soft cheek of the golden child.

"If it please you, my lady Queen," lisped Élisabeth. She looked at her mother, who nodded. "It is my greatest wish to be your damsel."

Marguerite smiled down at her. Élisabeth was tiny, but so perfectly formed, she seemed like a creature out of a fairy tale. "But of course, *chérie*. I would be most happy to have my little kinswoman at my court." As she gently tilted the child's chin, she noted the Duke and Duchess of York standing together.

"I had no idea the Woodville woman was related to the queen," York muttered to his wife.

"Only by marriage," replied Duchess Cecylee in clear, bell-like tones. She glanced at Marguerite, then lowered her voice, but Marguerite's keen ears were still able to pick up her muffled tones. "Did you see how patched and mended her gown was? It looks as if she has only one gown."

"She has no dowry," whispered York. "I received this morning a letter from Gloucester. He deplores her lack of dowry and has publicly accused parliament of having bought a queen not worth ten marks."

Marguerite stiffened as she gently took her fingers away from Élisabeth's face.

"Are you unwell, my lady Queen?" whispered Eleanor, Countess of Somerset.

"There is no point in standing here." Duchess Cecylee's clear voice carried over to where the Queen sat with her attendants. "Let us go, my lord. 'Tis clear we are not wanted." She swept off, leaving Marguerite staring after her.

York flushed, bowed to the Queen, and hurried after his wife.

"Do not mind her," murmured Alice de la Pole, Countess of Suffolk coming into the room with refreshments just as my lady York disappeared. "Many call her Proud Cis."

"I do not mind," replied Marguerite, lifting her chin. "She may be Duchess, but I am Queen."

Chapter 4
Pontoise, English France

"You must try harder to win her favor," hissed Richard as Queen Marguerite appeared at the top of the stairs leading into the great hall. "I'm depending upon you to become her friend. You can offer Nan to be her damsel, if you wish."

Cecylee fingered an emerald necklace. She should not have swept from the room like that, and she couldn't understand why she had been overtaken by such ill temper. She turned to Richard. "I thank you for your suggestion, but Nan is over young for that at present. Mayhap when she is older."

As Marguerite arrived at the bottom of the stairs, Cecylee sank into a low curtsey while Richard, bowed, murmured various compliments, and offered Marguerite his arm. Cecylee walked behind on the arm of William de la Pole, Earl of Suffolk, the rest of the English court following. Cecylee frowned as she caught sight of Mistress Élisabeth Woodville dressed in a gold and green silk gown, her shimmering hair streaming down her back under a matching cap of gold and green.

Richard took Marguerite by the hand as he placed her in the seat of honor to his right. Cecylee sat on his left, next to the Earl of Suffolk, while Alice of Suffolk sat lower down. Richard had ensured that Marguerite was furnished with a fork, a new-fangled implement that the French court had adopted but was not yet common in England. He took care to cut up the choicest pieces of meat into small morsels so that she could pierce them with her fork and eat in one mouthful. As he did so, he murmured various compliments.

"Our last queen, Catrine de Valois, was fair, but not as lovely as you," he remarked, kissing the tips of Marguerite's fingers with a flourish.

Cecylee had never seen Richard pay court to another woman.

Marguerite smiled and leaned towards Richard: "I have learned something of your history. Was not Catrine de Valois wife to King Henri, the one who fought us at Agincourt?"

"Indeed, yes." York picked up a flagon of wine, raised an eyebrow, and at Marguerite's nod, refilled her goblet. "His queen came to England to make peace, madam, like yourself."

"Tell me about England. Where do you live?"

York sipped his wine and smiled. "I have several residences, but my favorite one is at Fotheringhay."

"Foh-dring-hey." Marguerite turned the name slowly over on her tongue.

Suffolk laughed. "We will make an Englishwoman of you yet, my lady!" he bellowed, causing Cecylee to jump. He rose to his feet: "A toast to our queen." The other men rose also.

"May our queen live a long and happy life." Suffolk glanced at Richard. "And with no enemies to mar her reign."

"To our queen," roared the other men as they pounded the tables and drank.

Duke Richard sat down and took another sip of his wine. "That is my wish also, my Queen," he remarked softly. He put his goblet down. "Fotheringhay is dear to my heart. My castle sits on top of a tall hill around which the River Nene curls."

"It sounds lovely," murmured Marguerite as she ate a morsel of food.

"It would give me the greatest pleasure if you were to visit us there. I could show you the church tower I designed."

Marguerite stopped eating and stared. Cecylee watched the expression on her face. Does she think we English are uncouth and wild savages?

"Tell me about your tower," said Marguerite.

"I had it built ten years ago, shortly after I came into my majority," replied Richard, cutting off a small portion of the roasted duck now placed before them. He laid it neatly on her trencher, put his knife down, and leaned back in his chair.

"It is octagonal and commands a fine view of the surrounding countryside."

"Why did you make it octagonal?"

Richard laughed. "Perhaps because it is unusual. To my knowledge, the only other octagonal tower I know of is the Lantern Tower of Ely Cathedral. I did not want it to be round or square because that would have made it look like a fortress." He rubbed his forked beard. "I wanted something that conveyed elegance and grace, qualities that I fear we are sorely lacking in England." He picked up Marguerite's hand and kissed it. "But you will remedy that, madam, of that I have no doubt."

Cecylee's stomach clenched at Marguerite's smile.

At length, the ladies rose to escort the queen upstairs to her bedchamber.

"I wish to learn English," remarked Marguerite as she entered the dark room with handsome carved furniture and heavy draperies, "but what should I read?"

"Have you heard of Master Geoffrey Chaucer?" asked Duchess Cecylee.

"Does he make shoes?" replied Marguerite, indicating that the ladies should sit around her.

My lady York laughed merrily. "No, no," she replied as soon as she could. "Though I see why you might think so. One of his forefathers must have been a *chaucelier* or shoemaker, for him to have the name Chaucer. But you should read him. He writes in English."

"What does he write about?"

Duchess Cecylee's grey eyes sparkled. "If you wish to understand the English, read the *Canterbury Tales*. There you will find people of every station in life. It will interest you greatly."

"I believe Master Chaucer was your mother's uncle, was he not?" murmured Jacquetta, stroking her daughter's hair.

Marguerite winced.

Duchess Cecylee turned pink. "An uncle-by-marriage." She lifted her chin. "I am not ashamed to be related to the greatest poet of the land. In any case, I am not the only one here to call Master Chaucer relative. My lady Suffolk is his granddaughter."

There was dead silence as Marguerite looked from Duchess Cecylee to Countess Alice and back again. How was it possible for these great ladies to have relatives who were not aristocratic? This mixing of classes wasn't right. Peasants should know their place and not get above their station.

"My lady Queen," lisped Élisabeth, "would you like for me to bring you some lavender water?"

"A goodly suggestion," remarked Countess Alice, rising and curtseying low before Marguerite. "I fear you are greatly fatigued, madam."

"Perhaps I should say my adieux," murmured Duchess Cecylee, "unless you wish me to stay, my lady Queen?"

"I will see you on the morrow," replied Marguerite, and so Duchess Cecylee curtseyed and made her way back to the great hall.

Alice clucked her tongue as she directed the servant girl to stoke up the fire. Élisabeth fetched a bowl of lavender water while Jacquetta unpinned Marguerite's headdress.

"Soon you will be in England, and you will see things for yourself," said Alice. "Suffolk and I are blessed to have many good friends at court, like Cardinal Beaufort and his family, the Somersets." She nodded towards Eleanor Beauchamp, Countess of Somerset, and smiled. "The king favors them greatly. So you do not need to worry about the Yorks and what they think. They are not in favor at court. Indeed, the king has not seen his cousin York now for four years. And Gloucester, the king's uncle, has been much discredited due to the foolishness of his wife."

"What did she do?"

"The poor lady was very unwise—" began Countess Eleanor.

"Eleanor Cobham was indicted on charges of conspiring to kill the king by means of witchcraft," said Jacquetta.

Marguerite turned in her seat to look both ladies in the face. "Why does York support Gloucester then? Surely his behavior is most treasonous."

Alice sighed. "I do not understand York, save that he has a most unwholesome ambition."

"York is completely untrustworthy," said Jacquetta. "He thinks only of gaining power, as if he is not the wealthiest peer in the kingdom." She turned to Élisabeth. "Kneel, *chérie*, with the bowl just so. Now hand the queen a napkin."

Marguerite smiled as she took the linen offered by the eight-year-old and slowly dipped her fingers.

"And his wife is little better," said Alice. "She is not called Proud Cis for nothing."

"The Duke of York was most charming to me tonight," remarked Marguerite. "And I have heard it said he is talented at administration and an excellent general."

"He can read Latin fluently," said Eleanor.

"He is well educated and intelligent, I grant him that," said Jacquetta. "But everything he does is governed by ambition. Why do you think he has taken such care to win golden opinions in France?"

"Do you think he should be recalled to England?" asked Marguerite.

"Suffolk says there are others who could govern Normandy who are more loyal," whispered Alice. "You might want to suggest to the king, my lady, that it would be most wise to keep an eye on York—"

Chapter 5
Placentia Palace, Greenwich, London
October 1445

"I had to pawn my collar. And now I'm back in England, what thanks do I get?" Richard, Duke of York, set his mouth into a grim line. It was seven months since he'd met Queen Marguerite in Pontoise and two months since King Henry had recalled him from Normandy.

Humphrey, Duke of Gloucester, shook his head and set his wine cup down. "I see nothing good in the fortunes of England. The king is so easily led. I know not why he's not more like his father, Great Harry. You would think a great warrior would breed a more warlike son." His voice trailed off as he stared gloomily out of the window at the thick fog that pressed inwards.

Richard had known Gloucester since he was a boy. When Richard had arrived at court after the death of Cecylee's father, Gloucester, also of the Plantagenet line, had befriended and persuaded him to use his wealth and family connections to act as a counterpoise against the ambitions of Cardinal Beaufort. Richard studied the face of his great mentor: The years had not been kind. Age had thickened his small frame and his dark hair was nearly white. Small wonder, thought Richard, with all he has had to endure in recent years.

"I adored my brother, the king," said Duke Humphrey. "I'll never forget the day we fought together at Agincourt. He was my hero and I always considered it my sacred duty to further his war policies in France. His aim was to defeat the French and annex the whole of France to the English Crown."

"And I support you in that aim. I hate to see my labor in Normandy go to waste."

"I know, my friend. You don't know how much I appreciate your support. Without it I would be a lonely man indeed. Cardinal Beaufort, his great-nephew Somerset, and his protégé Suffolk are all against the war, and they are in with the king."

"And now the queen."

"And now the queen," repeated Gloucester. "It's been a little over six months since the king's marriage, and already you and I are left out in the cold."

York poured more mulled wine and took a sip.

"Have they given you a position on the king's council?"

"No."

Gloucester sighed. "Of course not. After what happened to me—"

"What happened exactly?"

Gloucester drained his wine cup and held it out for Richard to pour another measure. "I was doing what I've been doing for the past twenty-five years, campaigning for the continuance of the war in France. We were so near victory, and we could have done it if only the king had given us money. But Beaufort and his friends dominate him. I protested vociferously against their anti-war policies, I believe them to be a betrayal of everything Great Harry stood for. They didn't like what I said and set out to ruin my credibility."

He drained another wine-cup and slumped in his seat. "Around the time you arrived in Rouen, my lady wife was attending a dinner in London when she was arrested on charges of witchcraft. She and several others were tried. Her clerk was hung, drawn, and quartered. Her woman was burned at stake. My wife was sentenced to do three public penances, and then they shut her up in prison for life. I had to sit silently by, because they would have destroyed me as well. You have no idea what it was like seeing the lady you love being ruined before your very eyes."

Richard looked away. How would he have felt if Cecylee had been accused of witchcraft? He shuddered. Though Cecylee had wronged him greatly, he loved her still. One of the few pleasures in a life filled with duty was returning to the home she'd created for him. Richard always felt at peace when he saw her smile, inhaled her scent, and drank some concoction she'd prepared with her own hands. He didn't think he could bear it if Cecylee were shut up for life. It would be like quenching a candle flame. That was why he'd been unable to lock her up as she deserved. He couldn't quench her spirit. He looked up. Gloucester was blowing his nose on a handkerchief. "Was it true that Duchess Eleanor made a waxen image of the King?"

Gloucester sighed heavily, as he wiped his eyes. "My wife liked to dabble in witchcraft. She had her horoscope cast and it is true she made a waxen image of the king and melted it in a fire. But what harm could she do? The king is a young man in the best of health. Nothing my Eleanor did could alter that."

"But—"

"It was foolish, indeed, yes. And the poor lady is paying heavily for it now."

"But you continue to attend meetings of the king's council?"

"Not often. No one wants to listen to me because of this unfortunate business with my wife. They've discredited me, I tell you. This is all the doing of Cardinal Beaufort."

"Are you sure of that?"

"As sure as I can be. He's been trying to oust me from power for the past twenty years, and he's succeeded."

Duke Humphrey went to his bookshelf. He'd invited Richard into his private library where spines upon spines obscured the walls; he owned over two hundred books, more than any other magnate in England. "Now, where was it? I wanted to show you the latest work by Aretino." He put on a pair of spectacles and ran his fingers across the leather spines. "Ah, here it is. *The History of the Florentine People*, published about a year ago by the Republic of Florence." He gave Richard a twisted smile. "I wonder what you will make of this, my friend." He opened the book at a well-marked place and read:

> If one considers the savagery of Tiberius, the fury of Caligula, the insanity of Claudius, and the crimes of Nero with his mad delight in fire and sword; if one

adds Vitellius, Caracalla, Heliogabalus, Maximinus, and other monsters like them who horrified the whole world, one cannot deny that the Roman empire began to collapse once the disastrous name of Caesar had begun to brood over the city.

Richard threw back his head and laughed. "An apt comparison to the tyranny of our own times."

"My lord!" A messenger entered, wearing the badge of the falcon and the fetterlock, showing the Yorkist affinity. He was wet and muddy from a hard ride. Richard nodded, and the messenger came forward, knelt, and bowed his head. "I have ridden in from Westminster, my lord, from a meeting of Parliament to tell you—" He paused for breath. "To tell your lordship that Adam Moleyns, the Bishop of Chichester, has accused you of financial malpractice."

Richard's skin prickled as he blanched.

"No!" Gloucester whirled around, sending the book crashing to the floor. He jabbed a finger at the messenger. "This is a ploy to keep you off the king's council. Don't you see? Moleyns owes his bishopric to Suffolk. How dare they accuse you!"

Richard turned to the messenger. "What exactly did the bishop say?"

"He told Parliament that the campaigns in France were ruinously expensive. He said that so much money had been spent on Normandy, it didn't seem possible it could have cost that much. Either the Duke of York was foolishly overspending, he said, or he had pocketed the money."

A bead of ruby red liquid inched over the rim and dropped onto Richard's hand. He put his wine cup down. "How can he claim I pocketed the money when the King never paid me my annuity?"

Gloucester picked up his book and placed it on the table. "We must avenge this insult." He stormed downstairs, shouting for his horse. York hurried after him. Both lords mounted their horses, and set off at a fast gallop towards Westminster.

　　　York and Gloucester vaulted off their horses, tossed
their reins to the groom, and strode into Westminster Hall
where parliament was meeting. As the door closed shut, the
heat of the room sucked them in. A fire roared in the grate,
and familiar faces crowded the chamber. Richard waited for
the sergeant-at-arms to announce them, and for the Duke of
Norfolk to invite them to speak.

　　　"This charge would be laughable were it not so
grave." York looked around the chamber of Westminster
Hall, meeting as many eyes as he could. "I've always dealt
honestly with the Crown. When my uncle, the Earl of March,
died, the custody of those lands should have been turned
over to me because I was his nearest living male heir.
However, the Crown saw fit to grant my lands to Cardinal
Beaufort. As a lad of fourteen, there was not much I could
do about that. Seven years later when I reached my majority, I
was informed I would get my lands back only if I paid the
king the sum of one thousand six hundred and forty-six
pounds and six pence. I swallowed this insult and paid the
king in full. The king has not treated me so courteously.
When I was appointed lieutenant-general of France, I was
promised an annuity of twenty thousand pounds, which I
never received. I had to use my own personal funds to secure
Normandy. I have summoned my officers from Normandy
who will give you a full accounting of the money I have
spent. You will see that far from pocketing money, I am so
deeply in debt, I have had to pawn my collar to pay my
soldiers. The crown owes me the sum of thirty-eight
thousand, six hundred and seventy-seven pounds." York sank
down on the bench next to Gloucester and wiped the
perspiration from his forehead.

　　　The Earl of Suffolk rose. "Call Master Elbeuf." He
looked around the room as a round gentleman appeared,
bowed low, and declared himself to be the comptroller to the
Duke of York.

　　　"Let us begin," intoned Suffolk. "You say Duke
Richard arrived in Rouen on Saint John's Day in the year
1441. Tell us how much he spent that day."

It took several days for Master Elbeuf to explain to Parliament the details of my lord of York's expenditure while he was in Rouen, for he had kept detailed records. Everything that was spent between June of 1441, when Richard of York took up his position as governor of Normandy, and October 1445, when he returned to England, was laid before Parliament. When York's comptroller finally sat down, Suffolk rose. "Is Richard, Duke of York, guilty of financial malpractice or no? It is for you, my lords, to decide."

Richard bowed his head and covered his face with his hands.

"Where is Duchess Cecylee?" whispered Gloucester. "Surely your lady wife should be with you at such a time."

York smiled briefly. "Cecylee is breeding. We expect to have our next child in May. She has not been well and I did not want her to become upset."

"Indeed," sighed Gloucester. "You are wise to let her stay at Fotheringhay."

"I had to insist upon it," remarked York. "You know how my wife is. She loves being at court, especially now that our new queen has made it livelier. Cecylee hates being left behind at Fotheringhay. The country is too quiet for her."

Several hours passed. Finally, John de Mowbray, third Duke of Norfolk, rose. As premier duke of the realm, he was tasked with adjudicating this matter. "We have come to a decision." He bowed to Suffolk. "We find Richard Duke of York to be not guilty of the charge of financial malpractice."

There was a roar from Richard's supporters. Gloucester thumped him on the back.

"Indeed," continued Norfolk, "we find that York has conducted his affairs with great probity and thoroughness. We recommend that the Crown repay him his loan of thirty-eight thousand pounds."

Chapter 6
Westminster Palace, London
December 1445

"My dear lord. You must fulfill the terms of the treaty. Can you not see that?"

"My dear wife, sit you down and we will talk," replied King Henry.

He enclosed her delicate hand with his own as he drank her in. Sixteen-year-old Marguerite d'Anjou was the most ravishing beauty. She was small-boned and slender. Her russet-colored velvet gown clung to her well-turned waist and hips, outlining her lovely bosom. She had a well-cut profile, with high cheekbones and deep-set black eyes. They'd been wed for eight months, and he had yet to make love to her. His confessor had forbidden it, saying that lovemaking was a self-indulgent sport, and that he should not come near her any more than was absolutely necessary for the begetting of an heir. Henry had not dared to; One glimpse of his wife's naked body would send him into paroxysms of lust, and then his soul would be damned to the second circle of hell for eternity. For had not Our Savior Jesus Christ called on us to live chaste lives dedicated to God? Had he not commanded his followers to forsake all family ties?

"You agreed to return Maine and Anjou to my uncle, King Charles."

He started. "Yes, dearest, I did, but I have not informed Parliament of this matter."

Marguerite leapt to her feet. "You are King of England!"

King Henry moved his head from side to side, his forehead creasing into a frown. "They are not going to like it," he murmured.

"What do you mean? Who is not going to like it?"

She looked so lovely when she was angry, the color mounting those pretty cheeks. How he longed to cover those rosy lips with kisses. But his confessor had told him that he must sacrifice himself to a life devoid of earthly pleasure so that he could lead the English people to the gates of heaven.

The confessor continued the work of pious Richard de Beauchamp, Earl of Warwick, who'd been his guardian from the time he was nine months. De Beauchamp had made the arduous pilgrimage to Jerusalem. He had been heralded the "Father of Courtesy" by the Holy Roman Emperor. He had instilled in the young king the values of kindness and piety, and well as a love for education. Indeed, he had been so successful in training his young charge in kingly craft that Henry had taken a precocious interest in politics. As a lad of twelve, he had attempted to intervene in some matter, astonishing his councilors. They had roundly told him to avoid becoming entangled in court intrigue and swayed by those who would manipulate him for their own advancement.

"Who is not going to like it?" repeated Marguerite.

"Parliament."

"Does it matter? Are they not peasants?"

"There are two knights from every shire in the country," replied Henry, eyeing his wife. *Deo Gracias*, but she was lovely. However, it was becoming clear that she didn't understand English customs. The King of England could not ignore his parliament, unlike the King of France.

"They are peasants!" exclaimed Marguerite

"They represent my people," replied Henry as he fingered the s-shaped gold collar around his neck. That and the signet ring on his right hand were the only marks of distinction he allowed himself. Otherwise, he dressed in unfashionable round-toed shoes and robes of indeterminate darkness.

Marguerite started to pace. "The people. Who cares what the people think. You should return these territories now as you promised, or you will dishonor your good name."

Marguerite had been at the court of Charles VII for only a year. She would have been perfect as Queen of France, thought Henry. Instead, she was Queen of England, and someone needed to explain to her about English politics, as de Beauchamp had done for him. But de Beauchamp had been dead these six years. Henry frowned with concentration. It was all so complicated. Where was the best place to start? Should he begin with the duties of the king? But she knew all about that. Perhaps he should tell her about the humble folk. But she seemed not to be interested—

"You promised to cede Maine and Anjou."

"Yes, dearest, I did. But I have not informed all of my magnates. Gloucester and York don't know about this provision of the treaty."

Marguerite snorted. "You are king. What are Gloucester and York to you? They must obey their sovereign lord."

"Your lady wife speaks the truth, my lord King," remarked Somerset bowing low as he entered. Edmund Beaufort, fourth Earl of Somerset, was a gentleman nearing forty. Despite his graying hair, his appearance was pleasing, his charming smile showing he'd kept most of his teeth. "Gloucester and York are like yesterday's vegetables, rotten to the core. You need not worry about them."

Henry chewed his lower lip. Someone was always squabbling with someone else. "York is one of my most powerful magnates," he said slowly, glancing at Marguerite. As such, perhaps he should begin Marguerite's political education by talking about this cousin. "He owns vast tracts of land in Wales, Ireland, and thirteen English counties. He has inherited great wealth."

"You are his liege lord," said Marguerite.

"He could make difficulties," replied Henry.

"What difficulties? What could he do?"

"He could embarrass me," responded Henry, looking down and fiddling with his ring. "He and Gloucester together."

"What does Gloucester have to do with this?"

Ah, the list of things Gloucester had to do with this. Gloucester was his uncle and was regent of England before Henry assumed his majority. He championed the war in France. But beyond that, how could he explain to his wife that the King of England had to consult with his magnates on matters of grave import? He heard de Beauchamp's voice: "Never forget, my lord King, to consult your magnates. Woe betide you, if you do not. Your great-great-grandsire, King Edward III, was a master of consultative kingship, and he ruled this land peacefully for fifty years."

"Gloucester is York's mentor," said Somerset, his voice gradually making its way through the thicket of Henry's thoughts. "They are the best of friends. Gloucester has always championed the war in France. York backs him up."

"That may be so," said Marguerite. "But it doesn't mean you can go back on your word." She knelt before Henry, taking his large hand between her two small ones. "My dear lord, you must sign. Can you not see that?"

Henry patted her hand as he gazed into the middle distance. He really needed to explain these things to her, but the hour of nones was approaching, and he must go to chapel. Afterwards, he expected a visitor from Cambridge University to talk about his new college. Four years ago, Henry had laid the foundation stone for a royal college dedicated to Our Lady and Saint Nicholas, and he was most anxious to choose the provost and the twelve impoverished students who would study there. Henry had been pleased with his idea of having twelve students, because it was the number of Christ's apostles, but should he increase it? Education was so important, and there were so many impoverished young men who could benefit. Seventy would be a goodly number, for it was the number of early evangelists chosen by Our Lord Jesus himself—

Dimly, Henry became aware of a dull and fiery light. He sat up in his chair. Had he gone to hell? Surely not; he didn't remember dying. He looked up to see Cardinal Beaufort standing before him, his red robes vibrating against the gathering winter darkness. Now well into his seventies, Cardinal Beaufort supported himself by leaning on a stick. Henry motioned him to sit.

"In the matter of your marriage treaty," said the Cardinal, "I can only advise you to abide by its terms. If you do not sign, you will be breaking your oath, and you will ruin your reputation."

"And mine," said Marguerite from her seat on a low stool by the king.

The cardinal bowed. "And your reputation, of course, my dear lady."

Henry stared at the floor. Where was Somerset? Hadn't he been here? And when had Cardinal Beaufort arrived? How much time had passed since Marguerite had started talking to him about Maine and Anjou? Was it hours, or days?

The cardinal beckoned and one of his clerks came forward with the parchment. He dipped the pen in ink and held it out for the king.

Henry looked away. He wanted more time to think. The situation was complex.

"Sign it!" shrieked Marguerite.

Henry jumped. The cardinal raised his hand. "My daughter—"

"Sign it! Sign it!" she screamed at the top of her voice. She lunged toward Henry, snatched the quill from the clerk's fingers, wrapped Henry's fingers around it, and started to guide the movement of the pen to form a signature.

Henry sat passively, fascinated by her energy. It emanated from her in waves, like narrow golden haloes. Henry never felt energetic, except when he was consulting with scholars. Recently, he'd had the idea of establishing several grammar schools around the country, so that poor boys could be educated—

Cardinal Beaufort rose. "You cannot do that, my daughter. It is not legal by the laws of England. You must wait and possess your soul in patience."

Marguerite flung the pen down and jabbed her finger at King Henry. "You don't care what this does to me or my reputation. You sit there like a larded duck and do nothing. Meanwhile, my father and uncle are left wondering what kind of man is this Harry of England that can't even keep his word." She sank onto the floor, sobbing, burying her face in her hands.

I don't sit here, thought King Henry. I am filled with thoughts and ideas. Haven't I explained this to you, my dearest? He put out his hand to touch her pretty hair, but she had gone. He drifted into a sea of disconnected thoughts and images. When he came to, he saw the face of the French ambassador looming before him.

Marguerite lifted her well-defined chin and turned to Henry. "I have here a letter to the King of France in which you give a solemn undertaking to cede the territories of Maine and Anjou to my father King Réné by the thirtieth of April of next year." She laid the parchment in front of him.

Henry looked away. Now where was he? It took him such a long time to get through his thoughts—

"You are doing it to please Charles VII, the King of France, at the request of your wife," remarked Marguerite as she dipped the pen in ink and held it out to him.

Henry looked at her. She had a dimple in her cheek.

"Please, my lord," she said sweetly. "For the love you bear me."

Love. That was the word. How he loved his wife. And she wanted him to sign this document. Aye. It was the only way he could show her that he loved her, until he plucked up enough courage to take her to his bed. He picked up the pen and slowly signed his name.

Marguerite clapped her hands.

Silence descended. The next thing he knew, his wife was kissing his cheek. "Thank you, my most redoubted lord," she murmured.

Henry sank back in his chair, pleased that she was happy. Now, who should explain English customs to her?

Chapter 7
Eltham Palace, Greenwich, London
April 1446

"It is beautiful in London, my lady, at the queen's gardens in Eltham with the flowers so fresh after a shower," began Jenet.

"Were there any celebrations? It's now a year since King Henry married."

"There was a service of thanksgiving held in their private chapel. As soon as it ended, the queen asked my lord to walk with her in the gardens. My heart sank, for you know how the Queen is, she never keeps still—"

Cecylee had sent Jenet to spy on Richard. Well, perhaps that was rather a dramatic way of putting it, but just as she was about to give birth to her seventh child, a message came from the Queen asking Richard to visit her at Eltham on a matter of some importance. Richard did not know what the Queen wanted, and Cecylee could not go with him. She instructed Jenet to go.

Cecylee gave Jenet a long list of things needed from London for the new baby's christening to provide subterfuge. But privately, she instructed Jenet to wear nondescript clothing, not pretty hand-me-downs, to kept her head down, and to speak only English, hoping that Richard wouldn't recognize her when she followed him through the streets of London.

"After the queen asked my lord husband to walk in the gardens, were you able to keep up with them?" she asked.

"Fortunately, my lord wanted to sit. He looked tired." Jenet paused, and Cecylee nodded.

So let me tell you what happens next, my lady. The place where my lord and the queen sat is not far from the stables, so I was able to go around a corner out of sight, but near enough to listen.

"I am so glad you could come," said the queen in her high, bell-like voice.

Holy Mother be thanked, I thought, it will be easy enough to hear everything she has to say.

"I understand your wife is about to birth your child."

"Yes, Your Grace," said my lord. "If she is a girl, the duchess and I would like to name her 'Margaret' after you. Of course with your permission."

The queen clapped her hands together. "Another Margot!" she exclaimed. Then she got up and started pacing. "I have another matter I would discuss with you. You know, my lord, that one of the provisions of the Treaty of Tours is that the truce holds until July 1446?"

"Indeed, my lady."

"The King of France and I wish to bind together the royal houses of France and England. So, we propose to you a marriage between his daughter Madeleine de Valois and your eldest son."

There was a long pause and it seemed to go on forever. Finally my lord said, "You would like for Princess Madeleine to marry Edmund?" I know he said 'Edmund,' my lady, because his voice rises as he gets to the end of the sentence.

Next thing I heard was peals of laughter, followed by gasps of breath. Finally the queen managed to say, "Surely, mon duc, you cannot have forgotten your own son's name. I mean your eldest son, your four-year-old son called Édouard – is not so?"

Cecylee raised her hand to stop Jenet's narrative flow. Six-year-old Nan was tapping her arm. "Mama, they are arguing again. I have told Edward not to tease Edmund, but he just laughs at me and tells me to go away." She frowned. "Why can't they play nicely together?"

Cecylee felt her unborn baby kick as she laughed and kissed her daughter's soft cheek. Nan was going to be a wonderful mother. At six, she was already playing peacemaker to her brothers, trying to curb Edward's natural exuberance so that his much quieter brother got his fair share of playthings and attention.

"Do you see what I mean?" inquired Nan, pointing.

Cecylee glanced over to see four-year-old Edward stick his tongue out as he made a large hoop roll around the room by beating it with a stick, while three-year-old Edmund stood there, balling his hands into fists and crying. She beckoned to Annette de Caux. "Take the children outside, for it is fine enough to play. And make Lord Edward share with his brother." Edward rushed off, laughing in his boisterous way, followed more sedately by Annette, who held Edmund's hand.

"May I stay and listen to Jenet's tale?" asked Nan.

"No, my child," replied Cecylee stroking Nan's dark brown hair, which coiled down her back in soft waves. "Jenet and I have something private to discuss. But when we're done, I shall tell you a story."

"You won't be long, Mama?" she called as she skipped away.

Cecylee shook her head, smiled, and turned back to Jenet.

The queen continued, "I mean your eldest son, your four-year-old son called Édouard – is not so? Your French son, monsieur le duc.*" She pealed with laughter. "Not the other one, the three-year-old, what is his name? Edder-mund, so English. Oh, I cannot say it."*

There was dead silence from milord, but the queen seemed not to notice. She laughed again and then continued, "You know, Édouard is so charmant. *Don't you remember how he sang to me those songs last year? Why, he had not quite three years. And he looked so well, so handsome. Oh I think he would be the husband for the little* princesse. *She has only three years, but is already extremely pretty. I think that Édouard would want a pretty woman to be his wife, is it not so?"*

There was another pause, and then I heard a deep intake of breath. "This is a great honor, Your Grace," my lord said, spacing out each word slowly. "But I must give a little thought to it. Edward is only four years old." His voice trailed off.

The next thing I noticed, milord was walking right past me. He disappeared in the direction of the river. I peeped around the corner to see the queen raise her eyebrows.

"This marriage has the backing of Suffolk," she called after him.

But my lord seemed not to hear.

The queen lifted her elegant little shoulders in a shrug and turned to go indoors. However, she caught sight of me and frowned. I made a bob, as if I'm an ignorant wench who's never seen the queen before and mumbled in English, as your ladyship instructed. She relaxed and walked off. Obviously I can't have understood a word she said, since she and my lord have been speaking French.

As soon as she was gone, I ran after my lord, keeping a distance. He went to the river, where some women were spreading out their washing to dry. There's a pile of wet clothing that needs attending to. So I set to, and lay it out on the bushes. It is indeed a fine day.

Meanwhile my lord stormed up and down on the strand, saying to himself, "Edmund, Edmund, I want you to be my heir."

He was very loud, my lady. The folk by the riverside, the women with their washing, the fishermen, the tavern keeper, the barmaids, they all gaped, but one look at his fine clothing and aristocratic bearing and they left him alone. Fortunately he was ranting and raving in French, so they can't have understood him.

I edged closer, for he was muttering to himself now. "What can I give my son? What can I give my son?" I heard him swearing under his breath, he even called the queen something I should not like to repeat. Then he struck his fists together and roared, "By Our Lady, how these women torment me." He drew his sword and started whacking at the trees, hedges, weeds, anything that happens to be near.

Everyone edged back then.

"She told me who my eldest son was! I know who my eldest son is, but she had the temerity to tell me who my own son is!" He worked himself into quite a lather by now.

The groom appeared with my lord's palfrey, but he took one look at him and hesitated. I signal for him to wait.

"I have it!" my lord exclaimed, sheathing his sword and panting hard. "I will make Edmund Earl of Rutland. That title belonged to the first Duke of York's heir, and it carries prestige. It will be my way of letting everyone know that Edmund is my true heir. I will have to give that bastard something, however, to prevent gossip." He paced up and down, rubbing his forked beard. "If I give that bastard the title Earl of March, it will remind everyone of that troublemaker, the last Earl of March, who plotted against King Henry V and succeeded in having my father executed." He struck one hand against the other and gave a harsh bark of laughter. "My wife will have to agree, she'll have no choice." Suddenly, he noticed the groom standing there with

his horse. He stopped dead, got onto his horse, and thundered off. We didn't see him for the rest of the day.

Jenet paused to help Cecylee ease a cushion behind her back. She was so large now, she could scarcely move. She motioned for Jenet to continue.

"I am loath to tell you, my lady, in your condition."

"I want to know!" snapped Cecylee.

Jenet opened a jar of ointment and massaged Cecylee's feet.

I spent the next several days going to Cheapside, to visit the drapers, silversmiths, and haberdashers, so that I could get everything to furnish the new baby's christening. On the evening of the fifth day, I am just returning to our lodgings when the groom mentions that an unnamed visitor was ushered into the duke's private chamber.

I think quickly. It is nigh on vespers, evening is drawing in, and my lord has not yet returned. I go to the kitchen and bribe one of the cooks to let me wear a cap and a sack apron so that I look like a humble kitchen maid.

I pick up a tray of beer and make my way up the stairs. Keeping my face bent, I try out the local London accent on a dark-haired lady dressed in a red riding habit, sitting in a carved chair by the fireplace. She shoots me a sharp glance and then returns to her thoughts. What can Duke Richard be doing with her?

Next thing, I hear a thud of heavy steps and my lord shouting for his bath. I use the time to look quickly around the room for a suitable hiding place, mending the fire as I do so. Dipping a curtsey to the lady's back, I make my way to a small door leading to a spiral staircase that goes back down to the kitchens. I close the door without shutting it, wedging some material from my skirts into it so that it stays open a crack. Balancing the tray on my knees I sit and wait.

Eventually my lord enters. I hear him whistling to himself as he enters the room, and then the sound ceases abruptly. Perhaps he's been stopped dead in his tracks with astonishment.

A chair scrapes back. "My lord of York. I wanted a word with you about—a private matter."

My lord does not reply at first. He pours himself some beer, and then sits. "Yes?" His tone is terse, like that of a military commander.

"I bring you important news, for the which you will have cause to thank me."

My lord snorts, taking a gulp of beer.

"Your wife, Lady Cecylee—"

"What about my wife?"

"She is unusually broad-minded for such a great lady in her choice of companions."

"My wife is my private affair," says my lord.

"You are a great military man, Duke Richard," replies the lady sweetly. "But you have one weakness: your lovely wife. She has you wrapped around her little finger, doesn't she?"

The silence is taut.

"I think you should know who Lady Cecylee's lover was. He was the son of a blacksmith."

"No!" roars my lord. "He was a nobleman of the House of Savoy!"

"He pretended to be the Duke of Savoy's son, but he was not. He was only a blacksmith's son."

"How do you know that?" shouts Duke Richard.

"He came from the village of Blay, near Bayeux in Normandy. There is a merchant from Bayeux, at this very moment, awaiting you in the Blue Swan in the village of Greenwich. He knows her lover's family. Go you there, my lord. You will find that I tell you true."

Jenet paused and looked down. Cecylee tapped her on the arm. Jenet sighed.

My lord thrust the door open and shouted for his horse. He banged downstairs, each footfall getting fainter with each descending step. Shortly afterward, the sound of galloping hooves floated up through the open window.

My lord didn't return until dawn.

A while after the duke left, the door to the back stairway opened and the lady stood there, smiling down at me. It was Lady Lisette, your brother's wife.

The tray of beer glasses rattled on my knees.

"Blaybourne," she snorted. "What a stupid name. It's obvious it is made up." She signaled for me to stand and walked ahead of me back into the room.

I followed her, head held high and put the tray down on a table.

"As your lady's sister," Lady Lisette said to me, "I made it my business to find out more about her lover. I made some inquiries and discovered that there was a village named Blay near Bayeux. I sent my personal servant there, and he found Blaybourne's brother. He had an interesting tale to tell."

"My lady," I said. "Forgive my boldness, but what you did was not well done. It was not kind."

She slapped me. "Hussy!" she snapped. "Why shouldn't Lady Cecylee pay for her sins? She knows she's a sinner! Why, she's desperate enough to send her maid to spy on her own husband!" She laughed shrilly.

I rubbed my cheek.

She stared at me for a moment, and then smiled: "Perhaps you should warn your lady."

Chapter 8
Placentia Palace, Greenwich, London
April 28th 1446

Richard did not get much sleep for the next several days. Bad enough to have taken a lover—every time Richard imagined her in someone else's arms, his stomach churned. But to have lied? To have slept with a peasant?

A wine cup banging on the table pulled him out of his thoughts. As he looked at it, the ruby wine sloshed out, the cup skidded, and it fell to the ground with a clatter.

A servant scurried out to clear the mess, but Gloucester waved him away, went to his fireplace, and pounded the hood with his fist. "I don't believe it!" he roared.

Richard, Duke of York, sank back in his chair and wiped his face with the back of his hand.

A servant materialized with a bowl of water and a napkin for washing his face and hands, while another poured a full goblet of Gloucester's best claret. Richard downed his goblet and signaled for another. He nodded for the messenger to leave. He'd forgotten about this latest piece of treachery, he'd been so preoccupied with Cecylee. Really, he sometimes felt he barely knew his own wife.

Gloucester turned. "I can scarcely believe the king would do this. The English people won't abide it. We must go to court at once and learn the truth of the matter."

"What is this I hear about Maine and Anjou?" roared Gloucester, striding into the king's presence chamber, followed by York. He made only the most perfunctory of bows.

King Henry shrank into the cushions of his elaborately carved chair.

Queen Marguerite, however, rose from her low stool and stood tall, arms folded. "They belong to my father. It is part of the marriage agreement, is that not so, my dearest?" She turned to Henry.

"Yes," murmured Henry, moistening his lips with his tongue.

"It can't be true," said York, gazing at the King, who steadfastly refused to look him in the eye.

"It is," said Marguerite, lifting her chin. "My lord the king has solemnly promised the King of France that he will return these territories to my father by the thirtieth day of April."

"The thirtieth day of April?" stormed Gloucester. "You mean in two days?"

Marguerite nodded.

Gloucester paled.

"Does the council know of this?" asked Richard.

King Henry stared at the floor.

"What about the governors of Maine and Anjou?"

King Henry twisted his ring.

"You mean to say that you arranged this—these provisions of the treaty and told no-one?" roared Gloucester. "Not the council, not the governors, not the magnates, and least of all me?"

There was silence. As Richard studied the king, he saw the jaw twitch. Of course. This idea was too stupid even for King Henry. "Suffolk knew didn't he?" said Richard.

"And Cardinal Beaufort!" spat Gloucester.

"The Cardinal is a man of the church," said Marguerite. "You should not abuse—"

"This is absolutely breathtaking," shouted Gloucester. "I can't believe you would be so stupid. What? Give back the territories that we won under your glorious father? It can't be true!"

"It is," said Marguerite, coming forward, her eyes flashing. "And you, my lord, should mind your manners around the king."

"I have never heard of such addle-pated goings-on in all my days," shouted Gloucester. "You must be out of your mind!" He stormed off, banging the door behind him.

"Sire," said Richard, bowing low. "This is a most ill-conceived piece of diplomacy. Mark my words, you will live to regret it." He hurried after Gloucester.

Richard urged his palfrey into a gallop so that he could catch up with Gloucester, riding east to the city. What is he going to do now, thought Richard, following Gloucester along the Strand towards Saint Paul's Cathedral. As soon as they got to the churchyard, Gloucester vaulted off his horse, threw his reins to a groom, and mounted the steps of Saint Paul's Cross.

Richard followed.

The Londoners were enjoying themselves in the spring sunshine, it being that time of day after the main meal when people come out to pay visits, shop, and enjoy a fine afternoon stroll. In one corner of Saint Paul's churchyard, a number of well-dressed citizens fingered the leather covers and the crisp pages of those new-fangled printed books. There were goldsmiths and silversmiths. There was a woman selling spring flowers. There was even a horse merchant, whose restless charges stamped their feet, tossed their heads, and added a pungent odor to the scene.

Just outside the door of the church stood a group of London merchants. The soft leather of their boots and gloves displayed their wealth, as did the exotic and colorful material of their robes, their jewel-encrusted collars, and the many rings on their fingers. They were outdone only by their wives, who wore as many necklaces, rings, and brooches as possible crammed onto their costumes. Richard bowed to one beldame passing by. She had so much cloth in her headdress, her husband must belong to the clothier's guild.

As Gloucester arrived at Saint Paul's Cross, the people immediately began to gather, separating Richard from his mentor. "Good Duke Humphrey!" they shouted. "'Tis Good Duke Humphrey!"

Gloucester bowed. A tapster from a nearby alehouse ran up to hand him a mug of ale.

He looks years younger, thought Richard, glancing at his friend basking in the approval of the crowd. *How ironic that it is the people of England who respect him, not his aristocratic peers.*

The crowd gathered around Saint Paul's Cross, buzzing with excited anticipation as the horses neighed.

"I wonder what he's got to say," said the bookseller.

"I've never seen anything like it," said the flower seller. "Most of them fancy people never bother with the likes of us."

"Duke Humphrey, he's good," said the horse merchant. "He talks to us. Tells us what's going on."

"He's become a champion of good governance," said a well-dressed gentleman.

Duke Humphrey held up a hand, and the crowd fell silent.

"My friends, I have come here today to tell you about a piece of treachery. Nay, I can scarce believe it myself, and if any of you had told me this, I would think I had had a bad hangover from the night before."

Some youngsters in the crowd erupted into laughter. Their elders grew watchful and silent.

Richard accepted a tankard of beer and stood by Gloucester. He looked at the faces tilted up before him. *They don't seem overawed*, he thought, sipping his beer. *This country is not like France, where the common people grovel before the aristocrats. These people seem to know that their voices count for something.*

Gloucester raised his hand again. "Would you believe it, but in return for Margaret of Anjou, the Earl of Suffolk negotiated a marriage settlement in which we give away Maine and Anjou to the French."

The crowd recoiled. "No!" they shouted.

Richard grew uneasy.

"Yes, good people. Yes: I am sorry to tell you so, but there it is."

"What does this mean for trade, sir?" asked a man, a fashionably dressed woman on his arm.

"You lose the revenues from the counties of Maine and Anjou," replied Duke Humphrey. "You lose revenues from wine."

"Is our wine trade going to dry up?" asked one merchant with a red nose.

"Not unless we lose Bordeaux. So far, we are just talking about Maine and Anjou."

The crowd responded with a harsh bark of laughter.

"But I can tell you," continued Gloucester, "that the loss of Maine and Anjou means the loss of goodly fruit."

"No more pears!" exclaimed a young girl with golden hair hanging out from an upstairs window. "But that's my favorite fruit." Her high voice sailed over the noise of the crowd.

"No more Anjou pears, madam," said Gloucester sweeping her a low bow.

"Jacinda, do not shout out of the window. It is not ladylike." A woman with an elaborate horned headdress appeared and gently pulled the child away. "Please accept my apologies, my lord Duke," she called down. "She is very free."

"Do not worry, madam," said Gloucester bowing again with a flourish. "You have a charming daughter."

Applause and cheers greeted this remark.

"What about the landowners of Maine and Anjou, my lord?" asked a merchant dressed in fine crimson silk, rubies winking from the collar around his neck. "What about their lands and holdings?"

"A good question." Gloucester held up his hand to still the whispers and murmurings of the crowd. "They will be obliged to give up their lands. They will be forced to come home with nothing and start afresh."

The crowd erupted into boos and murmurs, which grew louder. Richard looked at his friend.

"I see you look puzzled, good people," remarked Gloucester, as the restless crowd grew silent. "Let me spell out the terms of the Treaty of Tours by which our king gained a wife. By this treaty, we give up Maine and Anjou. In return, we get exactly—nothing. That's right. Nothing. The queen did not even bring a dowry with her. Can you believe it? Can you believe that Suffolk would be so stupid, so asinine, so treacherous, as to throw away something that we gained in a fair fight for nothing in return?"

"No!"

Their roar threw Richard backward. He moved closer to Gloucester. "They're getting upset," he hissed.

Gloucester ignored him. "And all for a queen worth not ten marks," he remarked, holding up his tankard of ale. "I feel personally betrayed."

"We are betrayed!" roared the crowd. "A queen worth not ten marks!" They turned and hurried down Ludgate Hill in the direction of Westminster, shouting as they went.

"What are they going to do?" asked Richard.

Gloucester chuckled. "They are going to Westminster Palace, to shout insults at the queen."

Chapter 9
The Herber, The Strand, London
February 1447

Nine months later, Humphrey, Duke of Gloucester was dead. His great friend Abbot Whethamstead averred that he had died of natural causes, but my lady queen had put him under house arrest and charged him with treason on the grounds that he had spread rumors that Suffolk was her lover.

Richard dropped into a seat by the fire. "This is such a shock," he murmured. "I feel as if my sword arm has been cut off."

"Indeed." Salisbury sighed heavily as he took the seat opposite.

Richard stroked his forked beard and narrowed his eyes. "I like not the sound of this. It seems a trivial reason to arrest someone for spreading gossip. And Gloucester was a royal duke. He must have thought he was untouchable."

"One good thing to come out of this sorry matter is that you become heir presumptive," remarked Salisbury, "until the queen bears a son."

"Or until the king makes Somerset his heir."

Salisbury shook his head. "You have a point there, my friend. Without Gloucester, you have no one close to you on the king's council. What will you do?"

Richard sagged in his seat, his eyes on the flames that flickered before him. Life seemed as dark as the shadows of this room. Salisbury was right. He was completely alone. How was he going to protect Cecylee and their children? Nan was now seven years old. Edmund was nearly four, Beth was nearly three, and Margaret was going to have her first birthday in May. Then there was Cecylee's bastard son, who was rising five. "I have been away in Normandy these four years. Others have the king's ear."

"You have three daughters," remarked Salisbury. "You will have to marry them off."

"They are so young," sighed Richard. "Cecylee would never agree to it."

"Of course Cis is not going to agree to it. But you have to focus on the larger picture. Who's going to champion Gloucester's cause of good governance if not you? Who's going to speak out for the common folk, if not you? Who's going to inherit Gloucester's political mantle, if not you? But enemies lurk in the shadows."

"True enough," said Richard, fingering his beard. "I'll have to be more temperate than Gloucester."

"Indeed. He was known for his fiery temper. But you must also protect your family. Your sons are not old enough to fight."

"True," said Richard, thinning his lips. "And Fotheringhay is not well defended. Perhaps I should send them to Ludlow, which can withstand a siege."

Salisbury rose and clapped him on the back. "A good thought. It will keep them out of the way. Ludlow is a good hundred miles from London, so they'll not easily be taken hostage. If you put your best men on the garrison, they will be safe."

Richard nodded somberly.

"And you must think of forming alliances with those who have the king's ear. They would make suitable husbands for your daughters. There's Suffolk's heir, John."

"No, no. His grandsire was but a merchant from Hull."

"He's wealthy and powerful. And his wife is kin."

"True, but I'd have to be desperate to marry my daughter into that family."

"Stafford's heir and Northumberland's heir are already married. So is Shrewsbury's heir. That leaves only the Tudors. They are of a suitable age. Edmund Tudor is turning seventeen and his brother Jasper is sixteen."

"But they are loyal to the king, their half-brother," said Richard. "It is not likely I can persuade them to my cause."

"What about Exeter's heir? He is the same age as Edmund Tudor."

Richard looked up. "Do you think Exeter would be willing to follow me?"

"Yes. Granted, he has strong ties to the throne. But his ties are those of blood, not of dependency. He's not like the Tudors, who owe everything to their half-brother the King. Everyone in Exeter's family was born the right side of the sheets."

Richard touched his gold collar with the spear-pointed diamond, which he'd recovered once the king had paid the debt.

"If you take my advice, you'll see about it now," said Salisbury, "before someone else comes along."

Richard grimaced. "Your advice is sound, my friend. My fear is that it will grieve Cecylee greatly."

Salisbury smiled as he shook his head at Richard. "My sister is a woman. And women are not logical about such things. You should not worry overmuch about her reaction. She'll get used to it."

"Cecylee is breeding again. I am loath to upset her."

"But this is an opportunity for your advancement. Surely you see that? You shouldn't throw it away because of the whims of a foolish woman. Even though she is my sister, and I love her dearly."

Chapter 10
Fotheringhay Castle, Northamptonshire
March 1447

Richard held a special ceremony for Edmund to invest him with the title Earl of Rutland, while Cecylee's son Edward was allowed only to style himself the Earl of March, there being no formal ceremony for him. Naturally, nothing came of the match that Queen Marguerite proposed between Edward and the French princess.

Cecylee was warned by these actions that Richard was seriously displeased. But he had yet to do his worst. Not more than a month passed before he decreed that both children—then aged four and three—should be sent off to live at Ludlow Castle, deep in the Mortimer lands on the Welsh marches. They were to have their own household and learn the manly arts of war.

Then Richard wasted no time in arranging a marriage between the Duke of Exeter's heir and their eldest daughter Nan.

"Not Nan! She is a child! She has but six years."

"The match is a good one. The Hollands have royal blood flowing through their veins."

"But what kind of person is Henry Holland?" Cecylee bunched up the rich ruby fabric of her new velvet gown. "Though he's only sixteen, I like not what I hear of him. He's already gaining a reputation for cruelty, for riding his horses too hard, for tormenting his dogs. His people seem terrified of him."

Richard tightened his jaw.

She paced up and down, her skirts swishing in the rushes. She stopped in front of Richard. "I cannot believe you would do this. It is the height of folly to put Nan in his mercy."

He took her by the shoulders. His fingers closed into a vise-like grip. "Cis: You are fond of gossip. Holland will become Duke of Exeter when his father dies. He is as close to the throne as I am. This is a splendid match."

"It is not a splendid match!" she said hotly, enunciating each word. "You are taking Nan away from me to folk she does not know. Holland's mother has been dead these fourteen years. His second wife has been dead for eight years. There will be no ladies to take care of her. And she will become a stranger to her brothers and sisters. You have encouraged those greedy Hollands, allowed them to talk you into this marriage. They will have the revenues from all the lands that Nan will bring as her dowry now."

A vein throbbed near his temple. He came closer and snapped, "How dare you lecture me on my duties as a father when you so forgot yourself as to lower yourself with an archer."

She backed away.

"You lied to me, Cis!" He thrust his face into hers. "You didn't tell me your son was a low-born bastard, now did you? I would have sent him away if I'd known, to be brought up by humble folk."

She clenched her hands. It had never occurred to her that Richard might think she'd deliberately tricked him. She took a step forward. "He was extremely well educated. He studied at university. He had pleasing manners."

"He was a peasant!" roared Richard. He took her by the shoulders and shook her. "Take hold of yourself, Cis, and stop making excuses. You slept with a peasant."

"But Our Lord and Savior was not ashamed to go amongst peasants, so why should I—"

Richard let go, went to the door of the chamber and turned. "I need Exeter's support," he spat. "I have plans for the House of York. Nan is to marry Holland now, and I'll have no more said against it."

Before Cecylee could open her mouth to reply, he stalked out.

For the marriage feast, she dressed Nan in a gown of green silk embroidered in silver thread, complete with matching cap, under which Nan's hair fell down in long brown waves. Cecylee embroidered Nan's gown herself, stitching *Anne, Duchesse of Exeter* around the hem, as if the monotony of the embroidery could somehow soothe her feelings.

At length, the feasting came to an end and it was time for Nan to leave. Cecylee held her hand as they took the stairs for the last time to the courtyard where grooms waited with the horses and a litter for Nan, for she was too young to ride so many miles on horseback.

"Goodbye, my sweetest child," she murmured, stooping to kiss Nan's upturned cheeks. She squeezed Nan's fingers gently. "May God bless and keep you."

Nan's eyes grew round. "Mama, where am I going?"

"You are going to Exeter, to be with your new husband."

"But you're coming with me, are you not, Mama?"

Cecylee slowly sank to her knees before the tiny form and took Nan into her arms. She clung tightly and wept. It was a foolish thing to do, but she could not help herself.

Nan started to wail. "Mama. Don't let them take me! I'll be good, I promise. I don't want to go."

Richard walked up, his face thunderous. "Cis!" he snapped. "What are you doing? Why are you upsetting the child?"

She rose shakily to her feet, fumbling for her handkerchief.

Exeter came up behind Richard and glared. "Come now, child," he said roughly. "Leave off your crying. Be a good girl and get into that litter."

Nan edged towards her mother.

Cecylee's hand instinctively curved around the tiny fingers.

"I won't," said Nan, and stamped her foot.

Cecylee's lips curved in agreement.

Richard clenched his jaw and without a word grabbed Nan. He hoisted her up and deposited her in the litter. The curtains closed.

"Mamaaaa!" she wailed, her voice muffled by the curtains. "Mama! Mama!"

Exeter got onto his horse, followed by his son Henry Holland, Nan's new husband. He signaled, and the whole procession moved off, several knights riding alongside the closed litter.

"Mama! Mama! Mama!"

The wailing voice grew fainter and fainter as the entourage disappeared into the darkness of the oncoming night. Cecylee buried her face in her hands and sobbed. She did so right in front of the servants, it was beyond her power to do anything else.

At length, she felt herself being gently led away. She threw herself onto her bed and howled.

She came to with a throbbing headache and eyes that were sore from weeping.

"There now, my lady, this'll do you good." Jenet opened the bed curtains and handed her a potion of her own making. "It contains valerian root and chamomile flowers."

Cecylee rose from the bed. "I cannot go on. When will I see her again?"

"You are being sorely tried, my lady. But you must make your peace with it."

"Must?"

Jenet shrugged. "Well, you tell me, my lady. Do you have a choice?"

Cecylee sank onto the window seat. "I had little idea marriage would be like this."

"But you knew women lose their legal rights when they marry."

"It's so easy for you. You have more rights than I. You, at least, can choose your husband. I had no choice. Nan has no choice. I wish I were a peasant."

"Sip some of this my lady, please. It will do you a power of good. You must keep up your strength for the baby that's coming."

At those words, Cecylee drank some of the valerian and chamomile concoction. "Do I look dreadful?"

"Of course you do. Your husband has been cruel to you."

She drained the rest of the cup. "He's angry with me."

"I know, my lady. You've wounded his pride and his masculine vanity."

She grimaced as she leaned back against the window seat. Joan, Nan, Henry, Edward, Edmund, Beth, Margaret. She counted them like beads on a string. This baby was growing large and her back was beginning to feel its weight. If he was a son, she hoped that Richard would allow her to call him William after her brother Lord Fauconberg. "My marriage is past mending."

"I wouldn't say that, my lady. Duke Richard has not banished you. He spends a great deal of time in your company."

"But he sends my children away." Her eyelids started to droop. "I know I'm foolish about my children," she murmured. "But I cannot help myself."

"That is one of the best things about you, my lady," said Jenet taking the cup away and unlacing her gown. "How you love your children. 'Tis a pleasure to see."

Chapter 11
Dublin, Ireland
Late Summer 1450

"A messenger from London."

Duchess Cecylee and Duke Richard, in the middle of holding their daily audiences in the great hall of Dublin Castle, looked to the far side of the crowd. As the travel-stained figure wearily knelt before them, Cecylee straightened in her seat. It was nearly three years since Nan had been married off to Exeter, and during that time Cecylee hadn't seen or heard of her daughter. Her numerous pregnancies made it impossible to travel the two hundred and fifty miles between Fotheringhay and Exeter. Cecylee counted out her beads on a string: Joan, Nan, Henry, Edward, Edmund, Beth, Margaret, William, John, George. And so, Cecylee wrote to Nan. Her letters had been returned unopened. When Cecylee had begged Richard to allow Jenet to visit, he'd refused. He would never forgive her for having taken a lover. Ever since, Cecylee sought out anyone who could give her news of her daughter.

"How go affairs in France?" asked Richard, motioning the messenger to rise.

"Not well, my lord Duke," he replied bowing. "My lord of Somerset has handed Caen over to the French."

Richard recoiled. "What did you say?"

The messenger repeated it.

Richard shot out of his chair. "This is madness!" he stormed. "This means the end of English rule in Normandy!" He called for a scribe and dictated a letter to the King of England.

While Richard was preoccupied, Cecylee turned to the messenger: "Have you news of my daughter the Duchess of Exeter?"

The messenger shook his head.

"Find out what you can," whispered Cecylee, slipping him a sovereign.

A month later, he reappeared. "His Grace the King bowed to your wishes and summoned parliament," he began. "But after hearing Somerset's explanation, he decided to make him Constable of England."

Richard stared at him, the color draining out of his face.

Cecylee put her hand over Richard's. Turning to the messenger, she inquired, "What do the people say about this?"

The messenger bowed. "They murmur that Somerset must be the queen's lover, madam."

Cecylee flinched, but Richard laughed. "Small wonder they think that," he said. "Why else make Somerset Constable of England? I've never heard of rewarding someone for bad judgment. The queen must have made a special request. I must go home."

"My lord?" Cecylee looked searchingly into his face.

"Aye, 'tis time. While I struggle here to end the squabbles in Ireland, I see England spiral downwards into chaos. The people need me."

"But don't you need permission of the king?" said Cecylee, feeling the baby kick. In a few months, she would present Richard with another child.

Richard gave a harsh bark of laughter. "I fear matters have gone beyond that point. I must leave, and leave now," he replied, kissing her on the cheek.

And so, in the space of a few hours, Richard saddled up and left, taking the messenger and many others with him. It was not until he'd left that Cecylee realized she'd not had a chance to ask him about Nan.

Several days later, the messenger returned and was ushered into the solar of Dublin Castle, where Cecylee was packing up her gowns and jewels, surrounded by her women and children, for Richard had instructed his wife to make all haste in leaving Ireland. Baby George was suckling his wet-nurse, four-year-old Margaret was playing with Jenet, while seven-year-old Beth kept close to her mother. Though Beth was now the same age as Nan had been at her marriage, thankfully her father had said nothing about marrying her off. Cecylee hoped that the deteriorating situation in England would keep him occupied for many moons to come. She motioned for the messenger to rise. "How is my lord?"

"In good health, and spirits, my lady," replied the messenger, bowing. "He successfully crossed to Wales and rode to Ludlow. There, he mustered a force of four thousand men and marched towards London. He is in London now, seeking an audience with the king."

Cecylee sighed and crossed herself, praying that common sense would prevail and that Richard would be safe. Nothing had gone right for him in recent years. The queen, fearing him, blocked all of his attempts to participate in government. Instead of making use of his considerable talents, she'd appointed York to be the king's lieutenant in Ireland. The position sounded like a great honor, but Richard and Cecylee were both painfully aware that the queen had banished him from London.

"Have you news of my daughter, the Duchess of Exeter?"

The messenger hesitated and looked at the floor.

"You heard something?"

He coughed. "Yes, my lady. But nothing good, I am afraid."

"Tell me," said Cecylee, motioning Annette to take Beth and the other children away.

"I happened to have business in that part of the country, and so I rode over to Exeter Castle. It is a fine fortress, tucked into one corner of the City of Exeter, and the Duke of Exeter lives in a fine mansion within, so I am told."

"You did not go into the castle yourself?"

"Alas, no, madam. I was turned away at the gate. But it was nighttime, and there was a full moon, so I let my horse linger nearby and—" He ran his tongue over his lips.

Cecylee felt her unborn baby kick as she sank into her seat. "And what?" she whispered.

"I swear I could hear a cry coming from the castle."

"A cry? What do you mean?"

The messenger was silent.

She rose. "I insist that you tell me."

"It sounded like someone screaming."

Chapter 12
London
Late November 1450

Richard pulled his palfrey to a halt and turned his head at the clarion call. There it came again, and again. As the notes died away, Richard's ear caught the thunder of hooves, and around a bend in the road came a large group of riders bearing the badge of the lion. John de Mowbray, Duke of Norfolk, had arrived as promised on the outskirts of London.

"Well met, nephew Norfolk." York clasped hands with his powerful nephew-in-law, the son of Cecylee's sister Cath. As premier Duke of the Realm, Norfolk's opinion counted.

"How is your lady wife?"

"She is recovering from the birth of our son Thomas," replied Richard, nudging his horse into a trot beside Norfolk's. "The child is sickly, and Cecylee spends every waking hour nursing him."

The horses' breath rose up in a steam in the chill November air. It was two months since Richard had hurried back from Ireland to confront his cousin over the mismanagement of affairs in France. Henry had bowed to York's wishes and summoned Parliament to meet in London on November sixth.

As the procession wound its way through the narrow streets of London, the people of London opened their upstairs windows to look down on them. These upper rooms jutted out over the lower ones, and were so close in places that it was possible for two lovers on opposite sides of the street to hold hands. When the people saw York, they took up his cry: "A York! A York! A York!"

"I see you are popular with the people", murmured Norfolk. "How many men did you bring?"

"Three thousand."

"A goodly number. I brought a similar number myself." He motioned for one of his men to dismount and knock at the nearest house.

Presently, the casement window above was thrust open, and a dame with an elaborately starched white headdress, setting off her rosy cheeks, looked down on their company.

"I have no rooms, good sir," she said, when Norfolk's man explained what he wanted. "This house and all of the surrounding ones are taken by men of my lord of Somerset's affinity."

"There's not a bed to be had between here and Whitechapel!" exclaimed another woman, opening the casement opposite. "London's an armed camp. Why every fellow who fancies he can wield a stick has come here."

A child scampered into the street. York pulled on the bit so savagely, his horse reared. He quickly brought it under control. The child ran away unharmed.

"Holy Mother be blessed," said a dame, turning her head. "'Tis indeed my lord of York. Good e'en to you, sir." She dropped a low curtsey that made her head disappear below the sill of the open window. "May God prosper your cause."

York smiled and waved. "Did you hear what she said? I must find Somerset."

"Is that wise?"

"A York! A York!" chanted the people, thrusting open their casements and leaning over the procession.

"Garday loo!" shouted a maid as she prepared to heave a bucket of slops out of the window. "'Tis my lord of York," hissed her mistress. "Wait."

"Thank you, good madam," said Norfolk, inclining his head.

"Save your wastewater for Somerset!" shouted a voice across the way.

The crowd erupted into cheers and guffaws.

"We must do something about the money woes of this country," said Richard, pacing up and down.

"Certainly, my lord," replied Sir William Oldhall, picking up his pen. Richard had known Sir William for years, first as a councilor in Normandy, and latterly as his chamberlain. The House of Commons had demonstrated their support of York by recently electing Sir William to be their Speaker.

"The king's councilors are prepared to discuss fixing the income for the royal household," said Richard. "But we need to go further. I propose that we pass an *Act of Resumption* that returns the huge swaths of land the king has given away to his favorites for the past thirteen years."

Sir William stroked his beard.

Richard smiled. Sir William was a wealthy Norfolk landowner with powerful friends and relations. "Find out if public opinion would support this demand."

Sir William rose. "We should also get a promise from the king to restore law and order in the shires." He bowed and left.

"The seamstress has arrived with your gown," said Eleanor, now Duchess of Somerset, curtseying low before the queen.

Marguerite motioned her friend to rise.

Eleanor slowly straightened but would not meet the Queen's eye.

Marguerite sighed. Eleanor had been so kind when she'd first come to England, lending her money so that she could pay her sailors. But as her relationship with the Duke of Somerset had grown closer, the friendship with his wife deteriorated.

Marguerite could not really blame her. Like most aristocratic ladies, Eleanor had been married off as a child, but when her husband died, leaving her a widow at the age of twenty-three, she'd fallen in love with Somerset and married him secretly. But recently, Queen Marguerite had turned to her dearest cousin Somerset. Her great friend, the Earl of

Suffolk, had been murdered that spring, and the queen needed someone to take his place in her counsels and as leader of the Court Party. She and Somerset saw each other every day, and he was beginning to look at her—

Marguerite never allowed herself to criticize her husband. She placed him in a special category, for he was like no man she'd ever known. Every day, he devoted himself to his prayers and to his charities. He was the most kind-hearted and sweetest-tempered lord, denying her nothing. Except that he would not, could not, Marguerite corrected herself, give her a child after five years of marriage. And she so longed for a baby, not only for political reasons, but for herself. If only she could have a son, York would be put in his place, for he would no longer be heir presumptive. And if not the king, then who? Marguerite smiled until her gaze landed on Eleanor. She bit her lip as her lady-in-waiting gently put the purple velvet gown embroidered in crimson thread over her head.

Eleanor gave Marguerite her mirror and stood beside her to study the effect of the gown. It set off Marguerite's sculpted profile and made her look much older than her twenty-one years. Marguerite sighed as she studied her face in the mirror, noting a couple of lines around her mouth. "How old I look. Don't you think so, Eleanor?"

Eleanor, who was some twenty years older than the Queen, glanced at her mistress, then turned and gathered up the Queen's discarded gowns. Marguerite looked glorious, but she wasn't going to tell her that. She too had noticed the way her husband looked at the queen. "It is true you have not the freshness you had when first you came to this land five years ago," she said. "But you have been sorely tried, my lady. Especially this year."

Marguerite caught her friend's hand as she passed by. "You are so good to me, Eleanor. I do not understand why."

Eleanor reddened as she averted her face. She turned to the queen's dressing table and busied herself with clearing it, putting the stoppers back on the jars of rosewater, lavender water, and angelica water.

There was silence.

"How I miss Suffolk," sighed Marguerite.

"Have they apprehended the villains?"

"No, no. It is all York's doing. He is so powerful, he can do as he pleases. All he wants is to create trouble for me, and my most redoubted lord, the king."

"The government of this country should not ignore the people of England!" exclaimed York.

The cheering was so loud, it nearly lifted off the hammer-beam roof of Westminster Hall. On that cold and chilly November morning, the temperature inside the hall rose as more and more people squeezed in to hear what York was saying. Assembled at one end of the hall were the great magnates of the land at the high table on the dais. Around the walls and packed several men deep stood the men-at-arms with their quarterstaffs, their badges clearly showing their affinities.

Richard of York stood before the lords in front of the dais, half turned to face the people who were crowding into the hall below. There was a little space between the steps that led down from the dais and the body of the hall. In the front row stood all the important citizens of London, including the lord mayor and his wife and several prominent merchants with their wives. Behind these people were the people of London, looking expectantly at the almost stout figure with a forked beard pointing his finger at the lords on the dais.

"I tell you, the people make reasonable demands," continued Richard. "It is folly to tax them so heavily while royal favorites are richly rewarded. And not only that, these men - already bloated with wealth beyond the wildest dreams of any poor plowman or widow - do not have to pay taxes. Where is the sense in that? The country needs money, and so it should tax its richest citizens."

York's voice was drowned out in cheers.

"I ask this parliament to pass the *Act of Resumption* that requires royal favorites to return the land they have been given these past thirteen years, so that the value of this land may be used to get this country out of financial ruin."

Nan's husband rose. "My lord of York, you have given a most interesting speech. But I don't think you can expect these lands to be returned. It would be like asking your lady wife to return a present you'd given her."

Exeter laughed and the other lords laughed with him.

"I think we can dismiss these complaints," he continued. "They are trivial. What does an unwashed peasant know of land husbandry? I tell you these lands are in good hands, and they should remain so."

"You should not dismiss the concerns of the people so lightly," said York, reddening. He glared at Exeter. But Exeter ignored him.

"You should not be questioning the king's judgment," he remarked, smiling. "What makes you think you know better than our king?"

The hall buzzed like a hive of angry bees.

"What of the traitors?" bellowed someone.

"What about the loss of Normandy?" shouted another.

"Impeach Somerset!" cried a third.

At this, the men-at-arms providing protection for the noble families brandished weapons and shouted: "Give us Justice! Punish the Traitors! Give us Justice! Punish the traitors!"

Their voices echoed around that huge room, soaring up to the hammer-beams built in the time of Richard II and dropping down to the old stone walls built in the time of William II.

Richard of York pointed his finger at the lords. "I demand that you impeach Somerset. Now."

Marguerite bit her lip. From her chamber in Westminster, she heard the roar of the crowd. No doubt, York stirred more trouble. She wished she were back in France. Her youth seemed so golden and faraway, a lost time that tugged at her heart. How could people who smelled so bad she wanted to retch, who went around with lice-infested hair, open boils, and unseemly rags make things so difficult? Marguerite could not understand why anyone would bother to listen to them. Yet her husband was afraid of them, and York manipulated their opinions to his own advantage.

She must have spoken aloud, for Eleanor made sympathetic murmurs as she folded up the queen's gowns.

"It's so lonely being queen," said Marguerite, looking out of the mullioned windows at the grey, pillow-shaped clouds, that were scattering flakes of snow as if they were goose-down feathers.

"You are not alone!" exclaimed Eleanor, turning and glaring. "Your husband, the king, indulges your every whim. And you have my Somerset."

Marguerite stared. She had never heard Eleanor speak so disrespectfully. She opened her mouth to say something when Eleanor interrupted. "My Somerset," she said, pointing her finger at the queen, "is devoted to you. He would do anything you asked. Anything."

"My Queen."

Marguerite turned, and Somerset came swiftly forward. He knelt and brushed her hand with his lips. Marguerite's mouth curved into a smile, regarding her friend. Though he was old enough to be her father, Edmund Beaufort, now Duke of Somerset, had the looks and manner of a much younger man. She was so absorbed in gazing into his eyes, she barely noticed Eleanor whisking out of the room with nary a curtsey.

Somerset arched an eyebrow as he rose. "You seem troubled, my love."

"York is giving a speech before the Commons today."

"Ah."

Marguerite moved closer and placed her hands within his. "I fear for you, dearest cousin. I fear that he will try to destroy you." A tear ran down her cheek.

Somerset brushed the tear away with his finger and stooped to kiss her cheek. "York cannot touch me: I have your favor and the favor of the king."

"But he will try," said Marguerite, lifting her face to his.

He bent down and kissed her slowly on the lips.

A sound of mailed feet made them turn. A detachment of guards rushed into the room, followed by the Constable of the Tower, who unrolled a parchment.

"My Lord of Somerset, I hereby arrest you on charges of treason. I am bidden to take you to the Tower forthwith."

Marguerite recoiled. "You cannot do this."

"I have Parliament's authority," replied the constable, as the guards seized Somerset.

"I am your queen!" shrieked Marguerite.

But the constable merely bowed and escorted Somerset out.

Marguerite sank down onto a window seat, sobbing. She could not understand it. How could Parliament have more power than the queen?

Sir William Oldhall rose to his feet. "To the Duke of York!" he exclaimed, holding his wine cup high. "Today, he has set England on the right course—with the Duke of Somerset shut up in the Tower."

Applause and cheers came from the assembled company of merchants and noblemen finishing the splendid feast provided by the wealthy merchant who'd rented out his house to the Duke during his stay in London.

"Sir William Oldhall, My Lord Mayor of London, and Master Simon Eyre, who graciously provided his house to me and this feast for us today, I thank you for your hospitality and for your vote of confidence in me. We have much to do to root out corruption and waste in this land."

Richard told the assembled gathering about his plans: How he wanted to raise revenues by cutting waste, rather than taxing the poor. How he wanted to bring justice back into the land so that murderers could not escape their crimes by bribing local juries. As he spoke, people nodded. They smiled. Their confidence stoked his excitement. "We have impeached Somerset," he said, "and now let us turn our attention to other members of the Court Party who have profited so unscrupulously at the expense of the country—"

"There was a duke who went to the Tower, Inducas," sang the crowd outside, making Richard stop.

"Who loved a queen full many a day, in temptationibus," the crowd sang on, their voices muffled by the glazing in the windows.

"This queen was lusty, proper and young, Inducas
"She offered the duke a way out of jail, in temptationibus."

Richard strode to the window. Chairs scraped as the assembled company rose hastily and followed, thrusting open the casements. The crowd bubbled with shy merriment as they recognized Richard of York:

Hey hey, fiddle-de-dee
What kind of queen have we?
Loyal, loyal to those she loves
And she loves this duke.
Hey hey, fiddle de dee
What'll happen tonight think we?
Jump jump, jump into bed
And cuddle and kiss—

"Good people, what is this?" called Richard down to the crowd.

"Your bird has flown, my lord Duke!" shouted someone.

"Queen's got her lover back!" shouted another.

A messenger rode up and reined in sharply. The horse quivered, its flanks still damp from exertion. It snorted through its nostrils, sending great puffs of steam into the air. "I've come from the Tower!" he shouted, gasping for breath. "My lady queen went to the king and prevailed upon him to set Somerset free."

Chapter 13
1452 to 1453

Richard passed a hand over his forehead. The water trickling down his face was not from the rain alone. His show of force would be interpreted as an act of treason against the king.

He groaned as he slid off his horse. The past fifteen months had not been good. He hadn't been able to prevail in his plans for reform, and things went from bad to worse. Somerset, who just presided over the ignominious loss of Normandy, had been appointed Captain of Calais, the largest garrison maintained by the Crown. In August 1451, the entire duchy of Aquitaine surrendered to the French King. The merchants of England were shocked and dismayed, for in the space of two months they'd lost their grip on the lucrative wine trade that flowed through Bordeaux.

By summer's end it was plain to all that King Henry VI had no plans to implement government reform. France was all but lost, his government as rotten as a barrel of bad apples, justice was as scarce as hen's teeth, and disorder and anarchy prevailed. Yet the king was content to let things remain as they were.

York worked tirelessly for months, courting public opinion and sending his agents up and down the country to tell the good people of England that the king was fitter for a cloister than a throne. Then York left Ludlow and led his army towards London, intending to take the capital. The Londoner's response was to man the defenses, for they knew full well that supporting Richard of York would be construed as treason.

Finding London barred to him, York swung his army south, crossed Kingston Bridge and led his army towards Dartford. There, he waited for the king's army.

"My lord, there is an embassy come to speak with you from Her Grace the Queen."

Richard set his jaw. But he jerked up in surprise when a well-known figure was ushered in. "Salisbury!" he exclaimed. The Nevilles had been keeping distant from him during these campaigns against Somerset, and Salisbury had large problems of his own with the Percies.

"May I present my eldest son, Warwick?" Salisbury motioned to a tall, young man with fair hair. "And the Bishops of Ely and Winchester."

Richard snapped his fingers, and squires came forward to place chairs for his guests and to tie down the tent flaps, protecting the party from the soaking, cold rain.

The bishops sat, but Salisbury and Warwick remained standing. "I am come from the queen," said Salisbury, a member of the king's council, "to command you in the king's name to return to your allegiance."

York thinned his lips. "I have one condition: Somerset must be punished for his crimes against the state."

There was dead silence as his guests looked at one another.

Richard rose. "I will have the Duke of Somerset, or die therefore."

The Bishop of Winchester coughed. "Perhaps matters could be arranged to your liking if you were to have a private interview with the king." He looked at the Bishop of Ely.

Ely turned towards Richard, "I could engage Her Grace the Queen in a game of chess."

Richard smiled.

Next day, as Richard adjusted to the gloom inside the king's tent, the first thing his eyes lighted upon was Somerset. He jerked back.

Somerset bowed low with a flourish.

Another figure emerged from the gloom. It was the queen. She scowled.

Richard felt an icy finger crawling up his spine. Somerset was like a weevil who wouldn't go away.

"Welcome, my cousin of York," came the dull tones of the king's voice.

Coming forward, Richard knelt and kissed the king's ring. Then he brought out a parchment. "As you requested, my lord King, I have drawn up a the list of articles of indictment against my lord of Somerset."

The king nodded slightly.

Richard slowly unfurled the parchment.

"What's this?" shrieked Marguerite.

Henry slid his eyes towards his wife.

"Give that to me!" she screamed, making to reach for the document.

Henry sat stone still.

"How could you connive in this underhanded way with this—this viper?"

Richard took a deep breath and looked up. "My lady Queen, you do me an injustice. I am merely asking for the law of the land to be followed, and Somerset to be tried for his crimes."

"I am merely asking for the law of the land to be followed," sneered Somerset, mimicking Richard's lisping *r*'s. "Poppycock. You want power, my lord of York."

"My cousin has come in good faith to sue for peace," remarked Henry.

Richard turned to look at his cousin. Henry rarely stood up to anyone, least of all his wife. But Marguerite turned on him. "How could you go behind my back to your own worst enemy?" She jabbed a finger at Richard: "He's as cunning as a fox."

"He has the support of the Commons," replied Henry, but Marguerite was not listening.

"How could you listen to him? How could you arrest my dearest cousin to suit the whims—"

"He has the support of the people," said Henry. "That does count for something in this country."

"The people. Piffle," retorted Marguerite. "He goes on and on about the supposed crimes of our dear cousin. But what of his own ambition? I tell you, my lord King, York should be arrested. Immediately."

"No," said Henry.

The scene blurred before Richard's eyes. He'd dismissed his army. He'd come alone with only a few trusted retainers, believing he would have a private meeting with the king. How could he have blundered into this trap? Facing him, not two feet away, were his worst enemies. If they chose to arrest him—if they decided to try him for treason and execute him—Richard clenched his jaw as sweat trickled down his back. How was he going to get word to Cecylee?

An image of Cecylee filled his head, as he'd last seen her. She'd looked like a wounded bird. And they'd been arguing.

About Nan.

When Cecylee had returned from Ireland, she'd insisted, with a persistence and determination he did not know she had, that he allow her to send Jenet to Exeter to inquire into the health of their daughter. Richard had agreed; he would have no peace unless he did. Cecylee had packed up several boxes of things, medicines, Nan's favorite sweetmeats, even some things she'd left behind when she'd married Exeter, and sent Jenet off. It took her three months to return, bruises still visible upon her cheeks.

"I begged and pleaded, my lady, but he wouldn't let me in. Why, one of my lord of Exeter's men hit me in the face when I told him that your ladyship insisted that I see the duchess."

She rubbed a mark the size of a man's fist.

After Jenet had curtseyed and left, Cecylee had sat there silently, staring at the fire. It had unnerved him, to have his lively and talkative wife sitting there, unnaturally still. Finally, she'd lifted her head.

"You've killed her, Richard," she remarked before she stalked out and shut the door behind her.

He'd not been allowed into her bed since.

And now, as he took in his perilous condition, the hairs rose on the back of his neck.

"I'll send for the Constable of the Tower," declared Marguerite. "He is hard by."

"No," said King Henry.

Marguerite turned to pull the tent flap aside.

Henry rose. "I tell you no," he said loudly, his usually pale face flushed. "I agreed to arrest Somerset to be tried on charges of treason. He should be taken to the Tower."

Marguerite froze, poised in the action of leaving the tent. Her black eyes lost their sparkle as her face slackened. "You cannot mean that, my dearest lord."

She moved swiftly, knelt before the king, and took his hand. "What has he ever done to deserve this?" She covered her face with her hands and sobbed.

And so the king agreed to let Somerset go free.

"Your lord is in grave danger."

Cecylee stared at Sir William Oldhall. Richard? Danger? As she sagged into the cushions of her chair, she thought she saw Blaybourne standing before her: "Would you have me?" he asked. "I have always loved you, my love," she said, the words torn from her lips. "I will keep you safe," he replied, as his face dissolved into the face of her father. "I will lock you up," said Earl Ralph, "for you may be queen one day."

Someone touched her arm; Sir William's face swam into view.

"My lady," he said, touching her with a mud-splattered glove, "you look overwrought. Would you like me to come back when you have rested awhile?"

Cecylee came to with a jolt.

"What has happened?" she whispered.

"He has been taken prisoner."

Cecylee felt the color drain from her face. She'd been married to Richard now for fifteen years, and her lady friends envied her for the way he doted on her. She was never long out of his company. She traveled with him everywhere. She sat in on the various meetings he held. She held court with him in the great halls of various castles. She provided him with counsel in the privacy of their bedchamber—along with other pleasures, which caused her to breed nearly every year.

Her lady friends sighed as they talked about how lucky they were if their husbands merely ignored them. One lady considered herself fortunate that her husband was never around. Too often, husbands shouted at their ladies, or worse.

"You are so lucky, Cecylee, to have a husband that loves you," ladies exclaimed.

And Cecylee smiled, blushed, and turned the conversation into another current. For how could she explain that, though things had mellowed, there were still tears in the fabric of their marriage? Richard had never forgiven her for Blaybourne, and she had never forgiven him for Nan. Their marriage worked because they never discussed certain subjects, and also, thought Cecylee with a sigh of regret, because Richard still loved her. And now, she could not imagine a life without him. She counted out her beads on a string: Joan, Nan, Henry, Edward, Edmund, Beth, Margaret, William, John, George, Thomas.

"How many men can we raise?"

"Not enough to free him. His army is scattered to the winds."

"How can you be sure? We must be able to muster many men from our estates."

"We do not have much time, my lady," replied Sir William.

Cecylee set her lips. "We must fight our enemies some other way. We shall have to spread reports abroad."

Sir William glanced at her with a frown.

She placed her hand on his arm. "I am quite recovered from my shock, thank you, good Sir William. Let me explain. Since we cannot fight with an army, we must fight in the court of public opinion. The people of England should hear that my lord of York has been taken prisoner."

Sir William stroked his beard. Cecylee snapped her fingers and dictated to a waiting scribe:

Good People of England,

My lord of York, the People's Champion, has been arrested. My Lady Queen made him ride ahead of her in her train, as if he were a prisoner. She and my lord of Somerset have provided him with lodgings in the Tower.

Good people, I need your help in persuading Our Sovereign Lord the King to set him free. I enjoin you, therefore, to tell your friends and neighbors this news, so that we may bruit it abroad.

May God bless you for your efforts.

Given this sixth day of March, in the year of our Lord 1452.

By Cecylee, Duchess of York.

She signed her name and instructed a servant to ride to the collegiate church in the village of Fotheringhay and request the scribes there, in the name of their duchess, to make a hundred copies of the document. "While they do that, get a team of riders together, so that this can be placed in the marketplace of every good sized town."

The man bowed and left.

"Now master scribe, there is another message I would have you write. Make it in the form of a report, that a king's councilor would have. Put into this that Edward of York, Earl of March, has mustered an army of eleven thousand men and is marching on London from Ludlow. Say that he is gathering strength at every turn as the people rise to set my lord of York free."

Sir William shook his head. "'Tis fortunate that folk are not aware the Earl of March is a lad of only ten years."

One month later, the king issued a general pardon to all those who had risen against him. He graciously included my lord of York in this pardon. Four months after that, King Henry visited York at Ludlow Castle during his annual royal progress.

Duchess Cecylee was not there to greet the king, for she was lying some one hundred miles away at Fotheringhay, heavily pregnant with her twelfth child. When he was born, in October 1452, she named him Richard after his father, in thanksgiving for her husband's release. *Joan, Nan, Henry, Edward, Edmund, Beth, Margaret, William, John, George, Thomas, Richard,* thought Cecylee, as she lay in bed, recovering from Richard's birth.

Despite the king's visit, no progress was made in the furtherance of York's wish that his voice be heard on the king's council. Instead, early next year, Parliament authorized the king to be able to raise twenty thousand archers at a moment's notice, fearing that York would rise again. Alarmed, Cecylee decided to make a private visit to the queen around Whitsuntide, in the year 1453.

"What good would it do?" asked Richard. "She'll just laugh in your face."

Cecylee's grey eyes flashed as she thinned her lips. "Someone heard screams from Exeter Castle," she remarked coldly.

"You listen to gossip."

"The last time you said that to me, you forced Nan away from my side. The information I have comes from one of your agents."

"Cis, I'm so sorry—"

"Do you want me to help you, or not?"

"You're going to tell the queen I'm loyal and acting in good faith?"

"Exactly," replied Cecylee, lifting her chin. "She will be moved by my plea to show pity for the children."

He turned away. How could Cecylee be so naïve? The queen hated him. On the other hand, his lady wife was greatly upset about Nan; he wanted to comfort her. He tingled as she gently touched his arm. Since he'd returned from prison, she'd thawed and allowed him back into her bed. In return, Richard had made a private vow that he would not marry off their daughters before the age of consent at twelve years.

"Remember, Richard, she knows little of me," remarked Cecylee. "I believe I can persuade her."

"How can you persuade her when she would never believe me?"

"Because we have a common bond, being ladies of high station."

"I don't see how."

Cecylee put her small hand on top of his and lifted her face.

"You know the queen is expecting a baby. I shall take it upon myself to bring her such things as a lady in her condition might like. Then I can advise her—"

"I still don't see what this has to do with politics. How does your knowing about breeding make you persuasive?"

"I will catch her when her guard is down. She will be feeling vulnerable, anxious about the ordeal she is to undergo."

York stroked his beard, regarding her. Sir William Oldhall had brought a full report of Cecylee's cool handling of the crisis that had nearly cost him his life. He'd described her brilliant idea of fighting in the court of public opinion. "At first I did not know what she was talking of. Truly, I thought her wits had gone. But she was merely many strides ahead of me. You know how quick the duchess is."

Cecylee tilted her head as if she could read his thoughts. "I succeeded in getting you out of the queen's clutches alive."

He smiled as he bent to kiss his wife on the cheek. "So you did, my Cecylee. That was a deed well done. Well, if you believe you can shift her opinion—"

Cecylee smiled. "You agree that I should try?"

Chapter 14
Placentia Palace, Greenwich
Whitsuntide
May 1453

Marguerite regarded Duchess Cecylee with narrowed eyes. "It is most gracious of you to receive me, madam," murmured the duchess as she rose gracefully from her low curtsey.

Duchess Cecylee looked younger than her years. Wasn't she at least ten years older than Marguerite? How did she manage to look so slender after bearing so many children? How did she keep those roses in her cheeks when she was always breeding? Even her teeth were good, whereas she, Marguerite, was growing old. Every time she glanced at herself in her glass, she saw hard lines around her mouth and crow's feet around her eyes.

The truth was she'd done her work too well. Wedded to the King of England as part of the peace settlement between England and France, she'd been tireless in her efforts to further the interests of her countrymen. And she had succeeded brilliantly. First Maine and Anjou, then Normandy, then Aquitaine. All of these domains had fallen into the French king's lap because Marguerite wielded power over the English king and over his supporters Suffolk and Somerset. These men listened to her as she told them that the war with France would come to an end only if the French got back the land that was rightfully theirs.

The only person who stood in her way was York, and he'd stirred things up to such a fever pitch that even she, the redoubtable Marguerite, was disquieted by the hatred shown her by the people of England. Their stony silence, glares, and mutterings caused prickles of unease to run up her spine.

And now York's duchess had suddenly appeared. What could she possibly want? Was there some advantage to be gained here? She motioned the duchess to sit, signaling for wine to be poured.

The duchess sipped her wine delicately. "I am concerned about some things you might have heard about my lord of York."

Marguerite stared. She had expected the duchess to congratulate her about her pregnancy, dispense such advice she must surely have gained after bearing her lord twelve children. She raised an eyebrow. "I do not listen to gossip."

Duchess Cecylee flushed.

"I was not talking of gossip, madam," replied the duchess. She lifted her lashes to stare directly at Marguerite. "There have been some serious accusations made against my lord."

Marguerite rose and the duchess scrambled to her feet. Marguerite stared, but Duchess Cecylee met the gaze squarely. What would happen if Marguerite stirred the pot?

"I have heard it said that York is planning to attack the king. Is that so?"

"No, madam, it is not," replied the duchess immediately. She smiled. "Of course, my lord is not without his faults. He can be sometimes—difficult."

That is putting it mildly, thought Marguerite.

"You know how husbands can be," remarked the duchess, tilting her head on her slender neck. "But there is one thing York would never do, and that is break his oath. He takes these things very seriously."

She sipped her wine. "What mean you?"

"He took an oath of allegiance to your lord when he was crowned king. It would go against everything he stands for were he to break it now."

She frowned as she tried to concentrate. Suddenly, the dark room with its handsome furniture and heavy draperies felt unbearably hot. The baby kicked repeatedly. She drew herself up. "Your lord is ambitious. He is close to the throne. He has powerful supporters. Why wouldn't he try to gain power for himself?"

Duchess Cecylee sighed as she put her wine cup down. "Perhaps you do not know my husband as well as I thought. Perhaps you do not know he is deeply religious."

Religious? York? She'd seen him at Mass, but he seemed no more religious than the next man. "I always thought my husband was the religious one," remarked Marguerite as the room began to swirl.

Duchess Cecylee laughed, a bright tinkling sound echoing the bright points of candlelight that were making Marguerite's head ache.

"Well of course, madam, no one can match your husband for piety. My lord is not like that, but it does not mean religion is not important to him. Why, he prays every day, both morning and evening. He hears Mass with me every day. He visits our priest regularly—"

"Why are you telling me this?" she said, more abruptly than she'd meant. But she was dying for the duchess to leave so that she could go to her bedchamber and lie down.

"I want you to understand that my lord does not break his vows. Your lord was anointed king before God. My lord gave his oath of allegiance then. He is not some hot-headed young blade who would take power into his own hands because it suits him to do so."

"I see." Marguerite turned away to collect her scattered thoughts. But she was not feeling sharp today. She was aware that the duchess wanted something; there were undercurrents to everything she said. But today she could not fathom the depths. The duchess talked in riddles and her head ached. But before she let her go, she must exact a promise from her.

"So you are prepared, madam, to give me your assurances that your lord, the Duke of York, will never break his oath of allegiance to my lord, the king?

"Yes, madam. Just so," replied the Duchess, never breaking gaze.

Marguerite nodded slowly, as waves of relief washed over her. "I thank you for coming to tell me this, *duchesse*. It has eased my mind greatly, for I worry much about my lord —"

Marguerite's knees crumpled beneath her. She sank into her chair.

Duchess Cecylee smiled. "Let us think of more joyful tidings. You are going to bear your lord a child. I have brought some things to relieve the pain and discomfort of breeding."

She signaled and a maidservant appeared, bearing a basket full of herbs. Duchess Cecylee took out each carefully wrapped package.

"I have here chamomile to soothe the spirits, tansy to ease the joints, willow bark to cleanse the skin, and various other things that I think you might like to have."

She drew out a scroll of parchment. "I wrote down some things here, so that you don't have to remember. Breeding can be exhausting."

Marguerite motioned for the maid to come closer, so that she could see the contents of the basket for herself.

"Why, *duchesse*, that is most kind."

Cecylee patted her hand. "I have long experience in such matters, my dear. If I might be permitted to give you some advice—"

Marguerite nodded.

"Perhaps it would be better if you worried less about weighty matters of state and thought instead of giving your lord a fine and healthy son."

Marguerite bit her tongue on an angry retort. "Is there anything I can give you in return, my lady York?"

Duchess Cecylee looked down. "I hardly like to mention it," she murmured.

"Come now, you have been most kind to me. You have eased my mind. Is there anything you would like for your children?"

"If it please you, my lady Queen, I would like to have a pension of a thousand marks for myself and my children."

Marguerite's smile was genuine. So that was it. A request to buy York's loyalty. She would see to it immediately.

Chapter 15
Clarendon, Salisbury, Wiltshire
August 1453

What was he to do? Her belly had ripened like an exotic fruit. She was heavily *enceinte*—

Enceinte. Enceinte. Enceinte.

The word clanged in his head like a bell. King Henry closed his eyes.

It had been a warm day, but now he could feel cooler breezes touching his cheeks. Where was he? At his hunting lodge of Clarendon, outside Salisbury. It had been a beautiful day, and now it was evening. His servants bustled around, preparing a feast of roasted venison from that day's hunt.

Henry inhaled. The sharp tang of wood smoke mixed with roasted flesh assailed his nostrils. He shuddered. Henry left the hunting to others, preferring quiet rides through the forests where he could pray and meditate.

But now, what was he to do?

John Talbot, Earl of Shrewsbury and so greatly feared by the French generals, needed money. He'd swept through the region around Bordeaux, recapturing town after town. These successes were important for the English wine trade. It was important to support Talbot, Henry knew that. But something had happened—

"My lord King?"

King Henry blinked. His chamberlain, Richard Tunstall, bowed. "I have some goodly ale for you, sir. 'Tis a hot evening. Supper will be ready soon."

Henry nodded his thanks, and Tunstall bowed himself out.

Tunstall. Tunstall. Tunstall—had told him something. Henry frowned, clutching at an evanescent web of thought—

"The first comfortable notice that our most dearly beloved wife, the queen, was *enceinte* to our most singular consolation, and to all true liege people's joy and comfort."

Henry sank back into his carved chair and smiled. He'd remembered the message that Tunstall had delivered several months ago.

Now, what did it mean?

Henry frowned as the roots of his mind writhed. Men were like trees. And trees bore fruit. And Marguerite's belly was—like ripe fruit. Aye. She was bearing his child. She was bearing a child. She was going to have a baby.

But whose?

His?

Henry froze. Aye, that was the nub of the problem. He'd been trying to think of it for days, and here it was.

The baby.

Here it was.

Talbot. France. Aye, Talbot was dead. Aye, dead. Parliament had not voted Talbot the money. The King of France had invaded Aquitaine. With three armies. To Bordeaux. The French laid siege to Castillon. The English inhabitants asked Talbot to help. Talbot went to their aid. The French left. Talbot chased the French. They turned, pushing the English back to the banks of the Dordogne.

Talbot was cut to pieces.

With a battle-axe.

Henry put his ale down and rested his head in his hand. He pictured the Earl of Shrewsbury's murder. Not hungry. No. He could not eat roasted meat after that.

Henry closed his eyes. It was his fault. Henry's. He'd not given Talbot the money he needed. Now he was dead, hacked to pieces.

Bile rose in his throat. Sweat bloomed on his forehead.

They'd lost. Lost everything. In France. Everything his father had conquered. Everything they'd held for three hundred and eighty-seven years.

All gone.

Save for Calais.

Henry looked up. The sun was setting. A sunset. Sunset. Somerset. Somerset was a dear friend of the queen.

What should he do?

It was Somerset's. Yea: That was it. And he could not recognize a bastard. It was against God. But they would ask him, ask him. They would insist.

Henry half-shut his eyes. His magnates stood in front of him. They had huge, staring eyes.

"You must," they said.

"No," replied Henry.

They stared.

Stared.

"Disappear," said a voice.

"Disappear."

"Inside."

"Go."

On the fifteenth of August, the feast day of the Assumption of Our Blessed Lady, and around one month after the loss of everything in France, Our Sovereign Lord the King was at dinner in his hunting lodge of Clarendon, near Salisbury, when he complained of feeling unnaturally sleepy.

The next day, he went mad.

This piece of news was kept from Richard of York, for the queen and her councilors feared that on receipt of it, he would seize power. They were most alarmed by this turn of events. The king seemed to have taken a sudden leave of his senses. His head lolling, he spent his days in a chair, looked after by attendants. He could neither walk nor speak, nor understand, nor recognize anyone. It was as if he were in a kind of waking sleep. He was then thirty-two years.

The queen—determined to keep the condition secret —took the king to Westminster and summoned a horde of doctors. They tried everything, to no avail. The king was described by his physicians to be *non compos mentis*. Perhaps, they suggested, their sovereign lord was possessed by devils. Various priests were invited to exorcise any evil spirits, to no avail. The King was sent to Windsor, to live out his days in seclusion.

And so it came to pass, at a time that could not possibly be worse, that England lost her head of state. This event put an end to any hopes of unity—however slight—between the opposing factions of government. It brought Queen Marguerite, who little understood English politics, to the forefront of power. And it removed the last check on feuding magnates and on the rapaciousness of the Court Party.

On the thirteenth day of October, some two months after this catastrophe, the queen went into labor and brought forth a son she named Édouard, after King Henry's favorite saint, Edward the Confessor, whose feast day it was. The birth of the queen's son meant that neither York nor Somerset would be named heir presumptive. But at Windsor, the king was still in a stupor and did not even know he had a son.

That same month, the baby prince was baptized in a grand ceremony in Westminster Abbey. The queen did not attend, for it was not customary for a lady to appear in public after the birth of her child until she had been churched. As sponsors for the prince, the queen chose the Duke of Somerset, the Archbishop of Canterbury, and York's sister-in-law Anne Stafford née Neville, Duchess of Buckingham. My lord of York was not best pleased by the choice of Somerset to be a sponsor for the new prince.

It was around this time that rumors began to swirl like the dead leaves of November: Folk whispered that the new baby was not the son of the king at all, for who could imagine saintly, pious King Henry siring a son? Indeed, it seemed more likely that the baby prince was the son of Somerset, who was known to have a rather intense ... friendship with the queen.

By now, the queen and her advisors realized they could not conceal the king's condition indefinitely, for he showed no sign of recovering. The queen—whose motto was *Humble and Loyal*—did consider the possibility of allowing the king to abdicate in favor of his son, thus granting herself fifteen years of untrammeled power as Queen Regent.

Strangely, the lords of the council were unenthusiastic about this plan. But if not the queen, who was to be regent?

The birth of a son and heir necessitated the summoning of the magnates so that the baby prince could be formally acknowledged as heir-apparent to the throne. On the twenty-fourth day of October, therefore, Somerset, in the name of the queen, summoned such a council. York's name was omitted. This drew a storm of protest, especially from Norfolk, and so Somerset was obliged to invite York after all. When my lord of York finally arrived, he lost no time in gathering support against Somerset and the Court Party.

A little matter of the long-standing feud between the Nevilles and the Percies precipitated a change in the fortunes of my lord of York. Two things of note happened in the year 1453. In August, members of the Neville family were traveling to a family wedding at Sheriff Hutton when they were set upon by the Percies. This event drove the Nevilles—who had hitherto supported the House of Lancaster—to seek the powerful protection of York.

Another event confirmed this change of allegiance. Since the early part of 1453, Richard Neville, Earl of Warwick, had been involved in a bitter dispute with Somerset over the ownership of substantial lands in Wales that had formerly belonged to the House of Beauchamp, in particular, the lordship of Glamorgan. Warwick had held this lordship since 1450 and had administered it well. But early in 1453, Our Sovereign Lord the King, in his infinite wisdom, granted it to Somerset. Warwick fought for his rights and in the process realized what my lord of York had had to contend with all these years.

It so happened that York was Warwick's uncle-by-marriage, and Warwick himself was the most powerful Neville in his own right. This shabby treatment led Warwick to take sides, and whither Warwick led, so did the House of Neville follow. From the year 1453, therefore, Richard of York was to enjoy not only the influential support of my lord of Warwick—who was one of the richest and most powerful noblemen in England—but also of his father Richard Neville,

Earl of Salisbury, Duchess Cecylee's eldest brother. Together, York, Salisbury, and Warwick made a formidable team that would influence the course of events for the next several years. As M. de Commines was later to write: *It would have been better for the queen if she had acted more prudently in endeavoring to adjust the dispute between the Nevilles and Somerset, than to have said, "I am of Somerset's party. I will maintain it."*

Finally, my lord of York had acquired powerful allies among the magnates.

Chapter 16
October 1453

The queen could not keep the news of the king's condition hidden. Ancient custom demanded that the king recognize his heir, and so a deputation of twelve lords, spiritual and temporal, took the baby prince to visit his father. The cat came out of the bag as the sight of his heir failed to pull the king out of his strange state.

What to do? Parliament could not pass legislation confirming the child's right to the throne until the king acknowledged his son. The queen, who spared little thought for the people of England, found that her determination to conceal the king's condition cost her heavily, for folk interpreted the King's seeming hesitation as evidence that the baby prince was *definitely* a bastard!

Warwick wasted no time in making hay out of this predicament. He went before the people at Saint Paul's Cross one day in late October when it was fine but chill. London was bursting at the seams as all the magnates were in town to attend the christening of the baby prince, together with their servants. Folk scurried hither and thither, shopping for vegetables, for simples, for thread and bolts of cloth, at the grocers, the apothecaries, and the haberdashers, when my lord of Warwick appeared before them, dressed in a purple velvet cloak flung over a crimson velvet tunic. He stood tall in his black leather riding boots at the top of the steps leading to the cross, his long gloves slicing the air.

"I have come, good people, to bring you tidings from court in the matter of the queen's child."

A ripple of laughter went around the crowd.

"I know you must marvel at the king's hesitation." Warwick paused; the crowd rustled and went silent. It would have been possible to hear a needle fall.

"Why?" asked Warwick, his word as clear as a bell. "Why does the king delay in acknowledging the child to be his son?"

The question dropped into the cold air. The crowd rustled and came to life, as people turned to one another. Their murmurs grew louder and louder.

Warwick held up his hand. "One of two things is true about this child," he said. "Either he has appeared as a result of a fraud, smuggled up the backstairs into the queen's chamber after her own child died. Or he has come into this world as the offspring of an adulterous relationship."

The crowd roared with catcalls and whistles.

Warwick smiled and accepted a cup of ale from the keeper of the tavern hard by Saint Paul's Cross. The tavern stood empty as its inhabitants spilled out onto the street, sipping ale, cider and mulled wine, and dressed in everything from poor person's homespun to the magnificent furs and jewels of the London merchants and the aristocracy. The barman set up a line of boys to run into the tavern and get as many tankards of ale to the earl and his other customers as was needful.

"Thank you kindly," said Warwick to the barman as he quaffed the brimming tankard. "You brew the finest beer in London."

The barman flushed with pleasure at the laughs and cheers from the crowd. He signaled for more ale.

Warwick held up his hand and waited for silence.

"The king has not acknowledged the child as his son," he said slowly. "And furthermore, he never will."

There was a sudden intake of breath.

"It's true!" exclaimed a young woman, holding a twig basket that held a dried up turnip, a withered carrot, and some wilted sprigs of rosemary. Her high voice sailed over the noises from the crowd. As people turned to stare, she went bright pink.

"Holy Mary, Mother of Christ!" she exclaimed, blushing again as she crossed herself.

"Indeed, madam," said Warwick, stepping down from the cross, bowing, and offering her one of his cups of ale. "You put it well." He turned to the crowd as he remounted the steps of the cross.

"It is very shocking, is it not, that a crowned Queen of England, a queen anointed by holy oil, would stop at nothing to gain power? That such a queen, invested in spiritual power by the Archbishop of Canterbury, would lie to us? That she would stoop so low as to foist her bastard on us? What does she think we are, good people? Stupid?"

The crowd roared with laughter.

Warwick laughed along with them, and then he held up his hand. "Good people, we must be serious now, for things are not good in this land of ours. We've lost our wine trade, our cloth trade, prices are going up, and it is getting harder and harder to feed our families."

People nodded and edged closer.

"Now I am for the good of this country. I think this country should be prosperous and strong."

"Hear, hear!" shouted someone from the back of the crowd.

"But things must change," said Warwick. "Things must change for the better. And I want you all to know one thing. I want you to know that I will defend the interests of the people with all my power."

He looked around the crowd. "I will defend the interests of the people with all my power," he said again, and then bent down and seized another brimming tankard, which he held high in the air. "To the people of England," shouted Warwick, then quaffed it in one gulp.

"To Warwick!" roared the people, as they raised their tankards, wine cups, hats, hands and daggers.

"A Warwick! A Warwick! A Warwick!" chanted some apprentices at the back of the crowd, who then took up the chant.

Warwick smiled warmly and held out his arms.

The crowd silenced immediately.

"Now, good people, I know many of you go to bed hungry and that you don't have enough to feed your children. I have a surprise for you."

He paused and scanned the crowd.

Everyone's face was turned towards him.

"I would like to invite you to my house on the Strand, where I roast six oxen every day. There, you may have as much meat as you like, and you may carry away as much meat as you can, provided that it fits onto the point of one dagger."

By these means, Warwick won the affection and esteem of the people of England, who put their greatest faith and trust into his hands.

Queen Marguerite swore never to forgive him.

Chapter 17
Feast of Saint Anselm
November 18, 1453

The queen behaved as if the birth of a son consolidated her power and standing in the country.

On the eighteenth day of November 1453, around a month after the birth of the baby prince, all noble ladies were summoned to Westminster Abbey to participate in a magnificent ceremony for the churching of the queen. But Cecylee was too distracted to get caught up in the excitement, for she realized that after a span of more than six years, she would finally be able to see Nan.

Heart in mouth, Cecylee looked around the crowded room. Alice Chaucer, Duchess of Suffolk, was laying out the Queen's robe, which had been trimmed with over five hundred sables. She was helped by Eleanor Beauchamp, Duchess of Somerset, and by Anne Beauchamp, Countess of Warwick. The rising temperature of the room mingled the odors of woodsmoke, wet leather, and the slightly rancid smell of fur pelts as more ladies crowded into the room.

Cecylee made her way to the only casement that was open.

And there she was.

Nan.

Only her blue-grey eyes were recognizable, but even these had changed. Gone was the wide-open innocence of the six-year-old child whom Cecylee had last seen. In their place was a hard, shut-in quality, as if a portcullis had gone down.

"Nan," called Cecylee softly, as she came closer. "Nan. It is you, isn't it?"

She examined the pallid countenance of her elegantly thin daughter, trying to reconcile the sharply etched profile of this young lady with the soft curves of the seven-year old girl.

Nan didn't respond.

Cecylee scrutinized her daughter. Nan was magnificently arrayed in blue velvet embroidered all over with silver thread. Her brown hair was neatly coiled around her head. She wore a heart-shaped headdress with a translucent veil and the requisite number of jewels. Outwardly, Nan looked like a duke's wife. But her face was white, her eyes dull, and her clothes hung on her.

As Cecylee stared, Nan kept her eyes lowered, hands clasped in front of her, the very picture of a decorous noblewoman.

"What is wrong?" Cecylee whispered.

Nan favored her mother with one brief glance, before lowering her lashes again.

Cecylee's hands trembled as she eased her daughter into a private corner of the room.

"He mistreats you, doesn't he?"

Nan stared at the floor.

Cecylee gently tilted her chin with one finger, but Nan closed her eyes.

"My dearest child, I will take you home if you wish."

Nan turned away.

Cecylee twisted her hands together. Where was her daughter? She remembered how Nan had looked after her brothers Edward and Edmund. She remembered how she'd adored Chatelaine and wept for several days when the little thing had been killed. She remembered her smile.

"Nan, come home with me. I beg of you."

Nan remained silent.

"Nan?"

Nan stared at the floor.

"Nan!"

Not a flicker passed across Nan's countenance.

"Nan, speak to me please, my sweet."

Cecylee's voice grew louder. She took a deep breath.

Nan edged away.

Cecylee looked around the room. Her eyes lighted on Jacquetta Woodville, Duchess of Bedford, who stood by the fireplace with her sixteen-year-old daughter, Élisabeth, now

Baroness Grey after marrying Sir John Grey of Groby. Both ladies were admiring one another's clothes, exchanging morsels of gossip and child-rearing advice. Tears pricked as Cecylee compared their easy relationship with the difficulties she now encountered with her abandoned child.

Nan spoke. "Go away."

Cecylee strained to hear those softly spoken words.

"But I'm your mother!"

Too late—others were becoming interested in their conversation. Jacquetta lifted her head and turned, scenting out a morsel of gossip. She turned back to Nan, who stared at her with thin lips. Her expression reminded Cecylee of how her aunt Isabel—Richard's sister—would look at her, most disapproving.

"Please," Cecylee whispered as she touched the sleeve of Nan's gown. "Please let me take you home. I'll make it up to you, I promise."

Nan was silent. There was no expression on her face.

This was not Nan. This was what remained of her.

There was a rustle as Jacquetta appeared with Élisabeth in tow. With only the briefest of nodes to Cecylee, she turned to Nan. "*Chérie*, you seem discomposed. It would never do to spoil our lady queen's triumph, now would it?"

Her words were like a dagger, shredding Cecylee's heart. "There is no need—"

But Jacquetta ignored her.

"Come with me, my sweet," continued Jacquetta smoothly to Nan, "and let my Élisabeth help you find your place."

Nan rose obediently and allowed the ladies to take each arm.

Cecylee rose also. "Nan—"

But Nan had gone.

Tears blinding her, Cecylee sank onto the window seat. Had Lisette's curse come true? She buried her face in her hands, tears trickling through her fingers. She took in great gulps of air as her chest heaved. Gradually, the room became silent. Cecylee blindly felt for her handkerchief and looked up.

They stared back.

The queen had arrived.

Cecylee rose, curtseyed, and took her place at the front of the procession. She was first lady of the land. She grabbed one corner of the queen's train and held her head high. But the magnificent service was a blur. Cecylee could see nothing.

Chapter 18
January 1454

The queen returned to the political scene with great determination. Motherhood transformed her, and not for the better. She became fiercely protective of her son's rights and she aimed to crush the House of York. From that moment on, a bitter struggle ensued, not so much between the king and York, or even between Somerset and York, but rather between my lord of York and my lady queen. York had won over the majority of the magnates and would seize power if nothing were done. It was imperative Édouard be declared heir to the throne of England.

"We must take the prince to Windsor," said Somerset, kissing Marguerite on the lips when she expressed her worries to him. He bundled her into her warmest furs, handed her the baby, and they set off to visit the king.

"My lord King!" said Somerset, speaking loudly and slowly as they entered the king's presence. "You have a fine son. All you need do is bless him." He took the prince in his arms and knelt.

King Henry sat in his chair, dressed in a faded blue robe trimmed with ermine. He stared vacantly.

Somerset brought the baby close so that the child was nearly sitting in the king's lap. The baby prince, restless, kicked out, one slipper hitting the side of the king's leg.

The king started. His head lolled.

"Place your hand on the prince's head and declare him to be your heir, I beseech you."

The king drooled, and a servant hastily wiped his mouth with a napkin.

Marguerite took the baby from Somerset.

"There are evil people who would deny him his rights," she said. "There has to be a formal announcement that he is your son, otherwise York will seize power."

The baby turned pink and wailed.

The king stirred and turned in the direction of the sound. But his eyes were empty.

"Bless your son, my dearest lord," said Marguerite.

The king slid down in his seat as his head fell to one side.

"My dearest Queen, I fear he cannot do so," said Somerset, signaling for the servants to hoist the king up in his chair. He covered her hand with his own. "I grieve to tell you this, but we have to admit defeat."

Marguerite handed him the baby and rose. "I do not admit defeat." She snapped her fingers. "We'll ride for London at once."

She swept into her rooms at the Palace of Westminster, demanding that her scribe attend her immediately.

"My love," said Somerset, hurrying behind her. "What can you do? The king recognizes nobody."

"Many magnates are reluctant to support York's bid for the regency because it might look as it they were committing treason. So, I am drawing up a bill."

Somerset looked over her shoulder as the scribe wrote to her dictation:

> *Item the first, I, Marguerite, Queen of England, desire to have the rule of the land of England in its entirety;*
>
> *Item the second, I, Marguerite, Queen of England, desire to have the power to appoint the Lord Chancellor, the Lord Treasurer, the Lord Privy Seal and all such other officers of the land;*
>
> *Item the third, I, Marguerite, Queen of England, desire to have the ability to give all bishoprics and all other such benefices within the King's gift;*
>
> *Item the fourth, I, Marguerite, Queen of England, desire to be granted by parliament an annuity consisting of monies for upkeep of the king, the prince, and myself—*

Chapter 19
January 1454

My lord of York and others of his affinity learned of the queen's plans for herself and England when a large crowd gathered outside Warwick's London residence, The Herber, now a focal point of opposition.

"We won't stomach foreigners," they shouted.

Inside, Warwick met with York, Salisbury, and Norfolk. On hearing the crowd, he went to the window and opened the casement.

"I pray you, good people, what is the meaning of this?"

"Queen's got the whip hand!" shouted one.

"She wants to rule!" shouted another.

"That one's a manly woman!" shouted a third. "Doesn't like taking orders."

"Ooh!" shouted the crowd.

"We don't want her!" shouted a fourth.

"We don't want her!" chanted the crowd.

"My lord of Warwick!" bellowed a beldame dressed in a purple velvet gown and a plum-colored horned headdress, "are you aware the queen has drawn up a bill giving herself supreme power over England?"

Warwick paled, clutching the casement. "God's teeth!" How was it possible? Warwick employed many spies in the queen's household and had yet to receive this news.

The crowd roared with laughter.

York, Salisbury, and Norfolk hurried to the window.

"A York! A York! A York!" shouted the crowd, as York appeared.

"What mean you, madam?" bellowed Warwick, beckoning to the beldame. "How came you by this information?"

She sank into a low curtsey and beckoned to a young girl. "This is my maid Popelina, who has a sister who is washerwoman to the queen. Today, I allowed her to have the afternoon off to visit her sister."

Warwick leaned out of the window and beckoned. "Come closer. We'll not bite."

The crowd laughed and made way for a fresh-faced girl of around seventeen, who now appeared and bobbed a curtsey.

"Tell us your story," said Warwick.

"'T'was not more than an hour since, sir—I mean, my lord. I was just helping my sister make up the queen's bed with fresh linens. We were spreading them out on the bed and tucking the corners just so. The queen is very particular about the way her bed is made—"

The crowd guffawed with laughter.

"What did you hear?" asked Warwick. This information was fresh from the oven if it were less than an hour since she'd heard the queen speak.

"Well, sir. The queen was in the next room talking to someone—"

"Her scribe," put in the beldame.

"Her scribe. I heard her say that she desired to rule England."

The crowd booed loudly, then rustled with mutterings.

"What else did she say?"

"Something about making a chancellor and making bishops—and money. That's it. I was bending over a tuck and smoothing it down, and I was thinking, Holy Mother Above, the queen wants to be king. I ran off as soon as I could to tell my mistress, for she told me always to keep an ear out for anything the queen might say."

"And so I brought the matter straight to your lordship," put in the beldame, "for I thought you ought to know."

Warwick thanked her and with a nod sent someone to ascertain if the story were true. If it were, he would employ Mistress Popelina to turn down beds for the queen in every corner of the country.

The Lords and Commons were offended by Queen Marguerite's highhandedness and took note of the people's determination not to be ruled by their haughty and arrogant French queen. And thus many lords who might not otherwise have done so first began to support Richard of York.

In March of the year 1454, the sudden death of the Archbishop of Canterbury gave great urgency to the matter of a regency, for the archbishop's successor could only be chosen on the authority of the king. A regent was needed.

Before reaching their decision, the lords of the council made one last visit to the king to see if he showed any signs of recovery.

He did not.

And so they sent for the Duke of York, closest of the lords to the throne of England by reason of his descent from the second and fourth sons of King Edward III.

On the twenty-seventh day of March of the year 1454, the Lords in Parliament nominated Richard of York to be regent of England. He was to enjoy the same title and powers, and the same limitations on his authority that Humphrey, Duke of Gloucester, had enjoyed during the long minority of King Henry VI. The Lords decreed that York should neither have title of governor nor regent, but should be named Lord Protector and Defender, because it conveyed a personal duty of protecting the realm both from enemies without as well as rebels within. They further stipulated that if the king did not recover, the office of protector should devolve upon Prince Edward when he achieved his majority. As this would not happen for at least fourteen years, great trust was put in York's hands.

Chapter 20
April 1454

Richard of York bowed low, unrolling a scroll and
scanning it briefly, and lifted his head. "From now on, you
will reside at Windsor with your lord husband, the king."

"You cannot order me to do that."

York smiled. The last time he'd met the queen, she'd
held his life in her hands. Now, he held power.

"Have you not heard, my lady, that I am regent?"

Marguerite bit her lip.

"You will leave within the hour."

She was silent.

He turned to Somerset, who stood by, handling the
baby prince. "And you, my lord, will go to the Tower to
answer charges of treason."

"No!" shrieked Marguerite. She flung herself between
Somerset and York. The baby prince wailed.

Her extreme action took Richard aback.

"My lord of Somerset will be well treated in the
Tower. He will be tried by his peers in the House of Lords, as
is his right. There is no need to be hysterical."

"He's not going," shouted Marguerite.

York nodded and the Constable of the Tower entered
the room with an armed escort.

Marguerite shrieked again, the baby echoing her
shrieks.

York sighed. Why did she have to make things so
difficult? He was saved by Somerset, who put his hand on her
cheek.

"My dear lady and my love, be not so fretful. All will
be well." He handed her the baby prince: "See how fine our
prince is. No one can take that away from you."

"But they will try," said Marguerite, sweeping York a
look. "Oh how I know it. Already, York—"

Somerset took the queen's hand and kissed its palm.

York nodded, and the Constable of the Tower read out the indictment, charging Somerset with treasonable acts and summoning him to the Tower to await his trial for impeachment. Handing the baby back to Somerset, Marguerite leapt to her feet and seized the parchment.

"Of course!" she cried. "It is signed and sealed by the hand of York. Oh, he will stop at nothing to destroy you."

Somerset glared, handed the baby prince to the queen, and took the document. He scanned it and looked at York, who folded his arms and waited. By now, the room was filling with armed guards. He turned to the queen.

"Marguerite, don't take on so. You know I must go."

"There must be something I can do."

Somerset shook his head.

York signaled; the guards took each arm and led Somerset off.

Marguerite collapsed in a heap of tears. Richard waited. After she'd sobbed herself dry, he said, "You will leave within the hour. Your household will follow in a few days."

"The prince?" she whispered.

York paused and regarded her. Now she looked vulnerable and young. "The prince as well," he said slowly. "But once you reach Windsor, you will not leave."

"You can't do that," she replied rising. "I am queen."

"It is not seemly for a woman to meddle in government as you have done, my lady. You should spend your days with your baby and your husband. That is your place."

Marguerite stamped her foot. The baby prince woke up from his brief slumber and wailed.

"How dare you insult me in this fashion!"

"No one wants you to be queen, my lady," replied York. "Saving, of course, yourself."

He paused again and looked at her. She was as willful as Cecylee, but unlike his wife, York found that he did not care for her at all. Strange, for she was a handsome woman. "You will do as I tell you. This country is in a grievous state thanks to you. Now you will rest at Windsor and mind your family, as a good wife should."

He turned to go.

"I'll not consent to this!" screamed Marguerite. "You cannot treat your queen thus! I will not have it!"

York sighed and signaled to his marshal, who nodded. Several more guards entered Marguerite's chamber.

"I do not like to force a lady, but you give me no choice."

The guards surrounded the chamber, and one of them plucked the baby prince from Marguerite's arms and handed it to a nursemaid.

Marguerite screamed so loudly that Richard wanted to cover his ears. As his men hesitated, he nodded again. A couple of guards took her by the arms and dragged her away.

"I'll not forget this!" she shrieked. "I'll never forgive this outrage!"

"We have not a moment to lose," said York as he took his seat as the head of the king's council.

"Indeed," replied Salisbury. "There are the Percies in the North still harrying our lands. Something needs to be done to curb their quarrelsome nature."

"There is the matter of the Crown's finances," said York. "We need to make adequate provision for the king's household without incurring further debts or draining the exchequer."

"The position of Archbishop of Canterbury lies vacant," put in Warwick.

York leaned back in his seat. "I've thought of that. It's vital we have someone reliable and loyal to our affinity."

"Whom do you propose?" asked Norfolk.

"Thomas Bourchier, the Bishop of Ely, would be a fine candidate. He's brother to my sister's husband, Viscount Henry Bourchier."

The lords deliberated on this matter for some time, but finally agreed that my lord of York's choice was sound.

"What mean you to do about the Percies?" asked Warwick.

"I shall visit them next month," replied York. "While I am away, you, my lord of Salisbury, will manage affairs in London."

Salisbury smiled and nodded. One of Richard's first acts upon becoming regent was to install Salisbury as Chancellor of England.

"There is also Lancastrian disaffection in the north and the west, provoked by Exeter," remarked Warwick. "He must be curbed."

York winced. Nan's husband was proving to be difficult to handle. Moreover, Cecylee had returned from the Queen's churching ceremony brokenhearted, convinced Exeter was brutalizing their daughter, and had taken to her bed. Nothing Richard could say would comfort her. Only his successes of the past several months had caused her to smile at him again. Richard regretted once again arranging that marriage with Exeter. Exeter spelled trouble. He should be watched.

Richard said aloud, "I think it would be prudent to hold my lord of Exeter at Pontefract."

"But he's your son-in-law," exclaimed Salisbury.

"That may be. But he does not act as kin. His allegiance is to the Court Party, and he has made that very clear to me on a number of occasions. I do not have much choice. Exeter is dangerous."

Warwick nodded. "Holding Exeter at Pontefract does make him a hostage for the good behavior of his affinity."

Chapter 21
November 1454

"What is the news from France?"

Cecylee distracted herself by talking to the French Ambassador. The king's Lancastrian supporters surrounded her, eying her warily. These days, she spent all of her time at court, entertaining foreign diplomats. Fifteen months had passed since the king had fallen into his strange state, but he showed no sign of coming out of it. *Joan, Nan, Henry, Edward, Edmund, Beth, Margaret, William, John, George, Thomas, Richard,* murmured Cecylee to herself, as she walked along the corridors. She found that living in Marguerite's magnificent palace of Placentia, wearing bejeweled dresses, and being treated as queen could not stem her sadness, nor stop her sleepless nights. Every time she turned around, something happened to rub her wound raw. Jacquetta, Duchess of Bedford, had just left this very room after telling her that Nan would bear a child in the spring.

Cecylee had listened calmly, but as soon as she left, motioned to the French Ambassador to sit beside her.

"Ah, my lady York, the news is not so good."

Cecylee raised her eyebrows politely as she signaled for wine. If Nan were expecting a child in the spring, then she would be a grandmother before she turned forty.

"Do you mean that matters between King Charles of France and his son, the Dauphin Louis, have gone awry?"

The ambassador sighed. "You are too well informed, madam. Indeed it is a matter of grave disquiet that the king and his heir do not see matters in the same light."

How would Nan fare without her mother to help her? Cecylee leaned forward.

"Is it possible that matters might get worse?"

"I hope not, madam."

She sighed. Perhaps families were difficult for everyone.

"I think I can speak for my husband as well as myself when I say that I hope matters will mend in France. But what is your opinion of the situation?"

The ambassador coughed. "I know that many are anxious to prevent war."

She studied him for a moment. War. That was a strong word for a family quarrel. "So the king would send an army against his son?"

The ambassador recoiled. "I did not say that, madam."

"No you did not," replied Cecylee, signaling for a servant to refill the ambassador's wine cup. She would have to find a way of sending Jenet with a basket of herbs and things for her daughter's lying-in. "But it is a possibility?"

The ambassador sipped and coughed again, putting his cup down to speak. The arrival of her nephew Humphrey, Earl of Stafford, Anne's eldest son, interrupted them.

"My wife has given me a son," he exclaimed.

Cecylee started, jolted out of her thoughts. She signaled to the servants to refill the wine cups.

"Congratulations, my lord," she said, handing him a brimming cup. The Buckingham line would be secure. Cecylee kept her celebrations from seeming too joyful, however, as the Staffords were staunch Lancastrians. She silently wished she could be delighted by the birth of Nan's child. Perhaps it would not be a good idea to send Jenet to her. She needed to send someone who did not obviously come from herself, as such overtures would be unwelcome. She repressed the now familiar pricking of tears and looked up.

The lords eyed her.

"How have you named the child?" enquired someone.

"We have named him Henry, after the king," replied Stafford with a smile.

"Let us drink to that," shouted another. And before she could open her mouth, they raised their wine cups. "To the king!" they roared.

Cecylee drank also, hoping the gesture would be appreciated by Richard's rivals. As she took the wine cup away from her lips, she became aware of someone in the doorway.

It was Richard. He entered the room slowly, followed by Salisbury and Warwick. Many pairs of eyes in silence watched the triumvirate that now governed England. Richard took a wine cup offered to him by a servant, raised it, and said, "Congratulations, Stafford, on the birth of your son. To Henry."

The others raised their goblets and drank again.

There was an awkward pause.

"My lords," said York setting his wine cup down. "I request that you draw up ordinances for the reduction and reform of the king's household."

"What ordinances?" snapped Buckingham, not moved by the toast to his grandson.

"I have to reduce costs to avoid draining the exchequer."

"You have to—poppycock. This is aimed at our lady queen."

"Everyone will be affected," replied York. "There is no avoiding that."

"You must see, my lord of Buckingham, that the Crown has no money," put in Cecylee. "No one likes reducing costs. But it must be done."

Buckingham snorted.

"Our households are to be cut," said Edmund Tudor, Earl of Richmond, who stood there with his brother Jasper, Earl of Pembroke.

"And we are half-brothers to the king," put in Pembroke. "Our households will be only seven in number under my lord of York's plan. An entourage only equal to that of the king's confessor."

"How can you allow that?" exclaimed Henry Percy, Earl of Northumberland. "It's a disgrace!"

"We agree with my lord of York that such reforms are in our sovereign brother's interests," said Richmond.

"Otherwise, he would be destitute," said Pembroke. "Surely you've not forgotten the time when our sovereign king and his lady queen sat down to a feast at Epiphany only to be told by their steward there was no food to be had?"

Cecylee glanced at Richard, who was standing there silently. *This cannot be easy for him,* she thought. *He has to be so patient.*

Richard cleared his throat.

"I want you all to know that I have removed Exeter to Pontefract. He will stay there to cool his heels for a while."

Cecylee breathed deeply and smiled. *Maybe I can be with Nan after all.* She drew herself up and looked around her. The lords were standing there, stony-faced. "Let us pray," she said slowly, "that such reforms as my lord has wisely proposed be acceptable to all, for they are very necessary to the good governance of this realm."

Chapter 22
Feast of the Christ Child
Westminster Palace, London
December 25, 1454

Richard of York rose in his seat, lifted his wine cup high and toasted the king's health.

Duchess Cecylee and everyone else followed, saluting the king at a formal banquet that was hosted by York as part of the festivities for the Feast of the Christ Child.

Cecylee had just put her wine cup down and turned to congratulate Richard on the efforts he was making when a messenger rushed in.

"The king awakens. He awakens!"

A roar erupted as everyone rose to their feet and eyed one another. Without further ado, the entire court abandoned the Christmas feast and rushed to the stables calling for their favorite horses. Meanwhile, servants appeared with mantles of sable, fur-lined hoods, gloves, and boots to protect everyone from the winter weather.

It took the rest of the day to ride the thirty or so miles from the Palace of Westminster, where Christmas Court was held, to Windsor Castle, where the King was in residence. The entire court came in a rush upon the royal family.

The king sat in a high backed chair, smiling vaguely.

The queen knelt before him, holding her fourteen-month-old son Édouard. "See what a fine son you have, my King," she said.

"This child is heaven-sent," replied King Henry in a low, clear voice. "His birth must have been a miracle of the Holy Spirit."

The queen's face was a picture. She searched her husband's face, her own puckered in bewilderment. The entire court exploded into laughter. Truly, King Henry had returned to the land of the living, for only he would make such a pronouncement.

There was an awkward silence, then Warwick strode up. "This so-called prince," said he, jabbing a finger at the infant on Marguerite's lap, "is no son of yours, Sire." He bowed low before King Henry, then turned to face the entire court. "He's Somerset's son."

A roar of noise broke. Marguerite rose, clutching the child to her, who bawled lustily. "How dare you!" she hissed, spitting at Warwick, who took a step backwards. "You slander me with your lies, with your defamation. But I fight!"

She looked around the room. "I will fight you all if I have to!" She stormed out.

Cecylee was stunned. She knew the queen and Somerset were lovers, for Richard had told her about his visit when, as the newly-made Lord Protector of England, he had shut Somerset in the Tower and banished Marguerite to Windsor. Somerset had been holding the baby as if he were his own, and Richard repeated their conversation, complete with lover's words.

Now Marguerite displayed no guilt at her actions. Cecylee's never-quite-dormant anger welled up. How dare Richard manipulate her to feel guilty for her one night of sin? How dare he make her feel like an animal in a cage? She would be taken out for a petting once in a while, but if she bit, she would be thrust back in her cage, and the door slammed shut.

Cecylee took breath, and closed her eyes. What would happen now? Richard was no longer regent. She was no longer queen.

Chapter 23
Spring 1455

Though many wept for joy and declared the king to
be well mended, nevertheless he was not the same. His
strange illness left him at the mercy of his domineering lady
wife and quarrelsome nobles. From now on, royal authority
would be in the hands of a weak king, debilitated by a long
sleeping sickness that might recur at any time.

Events moved swiftly downhill after that Christmas
Day. On the ninth day of February 1455, King Henry
appeared in Parliament, whereupon he graciously gave thanks
to all present and dismissed my lord of York from the office
of protector. As soon as York relinquished his appointment,
Salisbury was dismissed from his position as chancellor, and
Exeter was set at liberty from his confinement at Pontefract.
Naturally, the queen lost no time in setting her lover free
from the Tower and restoring to him the offices of Constable
and Captain of Calais.

Upon hearing the news of Somerset's release, Richard
of York and others of his affinity rode out of London to
Yorkshire. York went to Sandal Castle, and Salisbury to
Middleham. Somerset already filled the king's ear with talk of
how my lord of York wished to depose the king and take the
throne of England for himself.

Through his numerous connections in London,
Warwick learned that Somerset was planning to hold a secret
conference at Westminster. Warwick urged York and
Salisbury not to wait to see what Somerset might do, but
instead to recruit an army. This they did without further ado,
and levies were summoned to muster both at Middleham and
Sandal, while Warwick began to assemble a large army of his
own at Warwick Castle.

Chapter 24
Sandal Castle, Yorkshire
May 1455

Exeter's return from Pontefract prevented Cecylee from attending her daughter's lying-in. She later heard that Nan gave birth to a healthy daughter, whom she named Anne after herself.

Perhaps it was just as well it was too dangerous to travel, mused Cecylee, sitting beside Richard on the dais of the great hall at Sandal Castle. Her belly swelled with her latest pregnancy. Joan, Nan, Henry, Edward, Edmund, Beth, Margaret, William, John, George, Thomas, Richard. This child would be her thirteenth.

It was May, and the door to the hall had been left open to allow in the fresh breezes of spring. Cecylee half listened to the stream of petitioners filing into the hall to discuss their problems with the duke and duchess, instead idly wondering if she would survive this latest pregnancy. A royal messenger bearing the leopards of Anjou and the lilies of France finally grabbed her attention.

"I bring a summons from my lord the king!" he cried, kneeling before Richard.

Richard frowned and tore open the parchment. His face went white.

"My lord, what ails you?" whispered Cecylee. She got to her feet slowly, heavy with pregnancy.

Richard handed the parchment to her. The king had summoned York, Salisbury, and Warwick to meet him before a great council of England to be held on the twenty-first day of May in the year 1455.

Cecylee scanned the document and bit her lip. She glanced up and signaled to the royal messenger to leave, then turned to Richard.

"My lord, you cannot go."

He clasped her hands. "You think as I do."

She stared into his grey-blue eyes. What will become
of the children if their father is murdered? I might not
survive many moons longer. "I well remember what
happened to my lord of Gloucester," she murmured under
her breath.

Richard set his lips, clasping Cecylee's hands within
his own. Then he strode briskly to the door and summoned
the messenger back into the room.

"Tell our sovereign lord that I am loyal to him and
that I will obey the summons."

The muscles of the young squire's face relaxed as he
nodded and bowed.

Then he left.

Cecylee smiled up at Richard. "You will strike first?"

"Exactly so." Richard bent and gave her a peck on the
cheek. "Take good care of yourself, my sweet," he murmured,
laying a hand on her belly.

York led his army southwards to London with the
intention of intercepting the king, the queen, and Somerset
before they left for Leicester. With him were Salisbury,
Viscount Bourchier, and others, which numbered some six
thousand men with their affinities. At the same time, Warwick
led an army of one thousand across England from Warwick
Castle to meet up with York and Salisbury on Ermine Street.

On the twentieth of May, York's army, now
numbering seven thousand men, arrived at the village of
Royston in Hertfordshire. While there, York learned that the
royal army was about to leave London without the queen,
who had taken the baby prince to Greenwich. On the twenty-
first day of May, the Yorkist army marched into the nearby
village of Ware. By the early hours of May 22, York's scouts
advised him that the king was making for Saint Albans, and
so York swung his army around and, just outside that town,
drew it up into three parts to be commanded by York,
Salisbury, and Warwick.

The royal army, numbering some two or three
thousand and commanded by Humphrey Stafford, Duke of

Buckingham, arrived in Saint Albans early on the morning of May 22. For three hours, York delayed starting the battle, making every effort to induce the king to listen to his complaints about Somerset's misgovernment. To no avail. The king sent back an uncharacteristically harsh reply.

"He refuses to accede to any of your demands," exclaimed Warwick.

"Somerset is behind this," muttered Salisbury.

York rose. "Let the battle begin."

So saying, he mounted his charger, put on his helmet, and ordered the trumpeters to sound the alarms. He rode in front of his troops and spoke.

"Today we stand at a turning point. Either we retreat to the misgovernment of the past, or we advance into the future, rid of all the traitors who would bleed the land white for their own gain."

"A York! A York! A York!" roared the troops.

"We have a hard fight ahead of us," shouted Richard. "I represent Job, and our Sovereign King is like King David, and together we will overcome Somerset."

The troops cheered, and the Battle of Saint Albans began.

York and Salisbury lead the charge from the East, along Saint Peter's Street, Sopwell Street, and other roads leading to the marketplace in an effort to storm the barricades the Lancastrian commanders put up to defend the town.

Many of the Lancastrian persuasion suffered that day. Henry Percy, Earl of Northumberland, husband to Cecylee's sister Alainor, perished in battle. Both Buckingham and his son and heir Humphrey Stafford was grievously wounded. But the big prizes were the death of Somerset and the capture of King Henry.

On May 23, 1455, York and Salisbury, preceded by Warwick bearing the king's sword, escorted our sovereign King Henry VI back to London, whereupon my lord of York assumed a new role as chief advisor to the king. He was immediately appointed to the position of Constable of England.

In the next week, the various members of the Court Party—Buckingham, Wiltshire, Shrewsbury, Richmond, Pembroke and some others—made peace with Richard of York. Pembroke was especially anxious to devise a way of reconciling all parties, and during the long hot summer months of 1455—while Cecylee waited for her youngest child to be born—he spent many hours with Richard discussing how best to achieve such a reconciliation.

But though Somerset was dead, his faction remained, and there was considerable bitterness amongst those who had lost their loved ones at Saint Albans.

Chapter 25
July 1455 to January 1458

By the beginning of July 1455, Richard of York had established himself as the effective ruler of England. As a mark of his newfound power, he gave Salisbury the influential office of Chancellor of the Duchy of Lancaster. Around this time, Cecylee gave birth to a daughter. Though she survived the birthing of her thirteenth child, the baby died soon after. Cecylee named her Ursula, in honor of Saint Ursula and her eleven thousand virgins.

Richard could not spare the time to grieve with his wife, for the king experienced another episode of his strange illness, and he assumed complete control of the governance of the country on the nineteenth day of November in the year 1455. Richard was once again appointed Protector and Defender of the Realm.

For the rest of the year, York and his allies formulated a radical program of reforms to bring order to the royal finances and the patronage of Crown lands. These ideas did not make him popular with the magnates. When King Henry regained his senses, these magnates surrounded him with complaints. In February of the year 1456, King Henry appeared in Parliament and—in a manner very similar to that of the year before—revoked my lord of York's appointment. He then ordered substantial changes to York's *Act of Resumption*. Despite this blow, York and his followers cooperated with the Court Party, and York himself remained a dominant voice on the king's council.

Queen Marguerite—who disliked Londoners—spent the spring of 1456 traveling around the country. While she was away, the king heeded York's advice and appointed Warwick to be Captain of Calais. This appointment was the most important military command within the king's gift. York was anxious that it should be given to Warwick to reward him for his crucial support at the Battle of Saint Albans. The queen had wanted to bestow this gift on Somerset's son and heir. By taking advantage of the queen's absence, York prevailed over the king.

With this coup, York allowed his guard to slip. He let the king go on royal progress around the country while he departed for Fotheringhay to spend time with his wife. The king went to Chester to reunite with the queen. With the king in her clutches, the queen prevailed upon him to dismiss persons of York's affinity from the government. Her plan was to throw York into the Tower and have him executed. But Buckingham persuaded her to banish him to Dublin instead.

Cecylee never forgot the way Richard looked when he came to her with news of this latest reprieve. Grey with fatigue, his expression made her bury any irritation. She sent him to Ireland with a kiss, promising that she would arrive soon. Then she went through the whole turmoil of packing up and organizing their trip across country from Fotheringhay, in Nottinghamshire, to Wales, where they took ship to Dublin. With her were fourteen-year-old Beth, twelve-year-old Margaret, eight-year-old George, and five-year-old Richard. At least the Irish had been right glad to see the Duke and Duchess of York return to Dublin, and so their sojourn provided some respite for poor Richard.

In January 1458, Richard of York was recalled to England by the king, who commanded all magnates to attend a peace conference at Westminster. Richard used the opportunity to forge new alliances.

"The time has come to marry Beth off."

"Couldn't she stay awhile longer? She is still young."

"Cis, we've had this conversation before. This is a splendid match. Beth will be Duchess of Suffolk."

"But first she will be the Duchess of Suffolk's daughter-in-law. Alice Chaucer, the present Duchess, is of hardy stock. She might last a long time."

"Beth will be with her kinswoman then, for you are related to the Chaucers too, my sweet." He put his arm around her waist.

Cecylee let him hold her for a moment, then pulled away.

"But I may not see her again," she said, trying not to sound too shrill. "I never see nor hear from Nan. She sent me no word when her daughter was born." She knelt. "Please, Dickon, I ask only for a few more years. Surely you could grant me that?"

Richard gently pulled her to her feet. "I cannot grant your wish. The marriage documents have already been drawn up, everything has been signed and sealed."

"Without my knowledge?" she flashed out.

Richard stiffened and his eyes went the color of steel.

"But why John de la Pole?" she asked, seeking to soften his gaze. "He is the son of your great enemy Suffolk."

"True," he replied, allowing the muscles of his face to relax. "But the son is made of different mettle than the father. Sir John has been loyal to the House of York." He clasped her hands within his own. "I nearly lost my life last year. I must use what time I have left to build affinities to protect our family. Surely you see that?"

Beth was married to John de la Pole within the month.

Chapter 26
1458 to1459

The next move in this game of chess came from
Queen Marguerite. Naturally, she wanted to oust Warwick
from the Captaincy of Calais, so she summoned him to
appear before the king's council to answer charges of piracy.

Her complaint stemmed from an incident in which
Warwick sent a small flotilla of ships across the channel, into
the Thames estuary to capture three Italian ships loaded with
English wool. The king himself had allowed the Italian
merchants to do this, but Warwick, ever attuned to the
feelings of the Londoners, sent his ships to get the wool
back. The king was unable to stop him, for he had but one
ship.

This exploit earned Warwick tremendous popularity,
for the London merchants, the source of so much of
England's wealth, were ignored and slighted by the
government. Warwick used his position as Captain of Calais
to put together a fleet of ten ships used to intercept
Burgundian, Hanseatic and French ships and to further
London's wealth. The Londoners regarded these deeds as
nothing less than heroic, but the queen was not best pleased.

If the queen believed she could get rid of Warwick
easily, she was to be disappointed. Warwick responded to her
summons by arriving in London in July 1458 at the head of
six hundred armed men. When the queen tried to press
charges, Warwick protested he was being treated unfairly. His
protests encouraged his supporters, of which there were
many, to run riot in London.

In the melee, the Attorney General was murdered.

Over the next several months, various scuffles broke
out between Warwick's supporters and those of the Court
Party. When the queen persuaded the council to draw up a
warrant for his arrest and committal to the Tower, he realized
it was no longer safe to remain in England. Warwick—whose
motto was *Seulement En*, or 'One Against Many'—returned to

Calais, remaining a continuous thorn in the queen's side. Marguerite was now determined to take decisive action, and in the latter months of 1458, she left London to raise an army.

Richard responded to the deteriorating situation by deciding that Fotheringhay Castle was no longer safe. As soon as the winter frosts melted away, heralding in the spring of 1459, Cecylee packed up the household and they left for Ludlow, which had stronger fortifications. With them went the younger remaining children: Margaret, thirteen; George, nine; and Richard, six.

Cecylee had seen scarcely anything of Edward during his childhood and young manhood, for Richard had packed him off to Ludlow at the age of four to provide company for his three-year-old half-brother Rutland, groomed to be the Yorkist heir. With the storms of Richard's political life and thirteen pregnancies, Cecylee could make only rare visits to Ludlow, for Fotheringhay Castle was a distance of one hundred and twenty-five miles away.

So when she entered the great hall at Ludlow Castle and a young man came towards her, Cecylee's heart stilled. He wore a tight tunic of dark blue velvet trimmed with gold thread. His long legs were encased in stockings that were half blue, half gold, with the seam up the middle of each leg. He was tall. His hair was golden, and his dark blue eyes were sharp with intelligence. His tunic ended at the hip, showing off legs that were long and very shapely.

He knelt down and kissed her hand. She froze.

"Madam. Mother. You look unwell. May I get something for you?"

He signaled for a servant to bring a chair. As he poured a cup of wine, he peered at her anxiously.

"You look as if you've seen a ghost," continued the young man.

"I have," she murmured, slowly sipping the wine he'd given her. For there, standing before her, was the veritable image of Blaybourne.

Cecylee glanced at Richard, who quickly understood. His expression hardened.

Ignoring Edward, he turned to the young man standing quietly by. It was then that Cecylee noticed her other son, Edmund, Earl of Rutland, aged sixteen years. Though he was tall like Edward, he greatly resembled Richard.

"Well met, my son," said Richard a little too loudly as he put his hand on Rutland's shoulder.

Rutland's pale face lit up into a smile.

"Let's go to the stables to pick out a fine stallion for you, my son," said Richard, with just the slightest emphasis on the repetition. He steered Rutland away from Edward. They disappeared outside and did not return for the rest of the day.

Richard spent much time with Rutland as they settled in, personally supervising his training in the art of warfare, while Cecylee was thrown into the company of her eldest son. She hadn't realized how much she longed for Blaybourne until then. Edward was very much like his father, not only in looks but also in wit. Although it was hard—even for his mother—not to notice he already boasted a notorious reputation for womanizing, Cecylee stopped her ears.

Edward was beguiling. He was charming. He made her feel that she was at the center of his life.

This gave her a confidence about him she should not have had.

One incident struck a discordant note. As she was eating a light supper with the younger children, Richard came in hot and flushed. He made a gesture with his thumb and forefinger to let her know that he wished to speak with her privately.

She nodded to Jenet and left.

When she entered Richard's private dressing room, Edward was there.

"Where is he?" Richard asked angrily.

"My lord, I am truly sorry. I cannot remember—"

"You cannot remember?" thundered Richard.

Cecylee put a hand on Richard's sleeve. "Edward. What has happened?"

He went down on one knee. "My lady mother, I crave your pardon, and that of my lord father."

Richard bristled but said nothing.

"Rutland and I were out riding when my horse went lame. He agreed to let me ride his horse. I am not sure where I left him."

"Edward," exclaimed Cecylee, "how can this be? Gentlemen are trained to know always where they are. How can you successfully win battles otherwise?"

He hung his head.

Cecylee looked at Richard, staring at her with a grim countenance.

"He does not know because he was drunk at the time, is that not so, you oaf?"

He poked Edward with the toe of his boot.

Edward stared at the floor.

"He promised to ride straight back to me," said Richard. "And then to bring Rutland a new horse. Instead he delayed, chasing wenches, is that not so?"

Cecylee's cheeks grew warm.

"I found him," continued Richard, "in a local stew, sodden with drink. When, finally, I roused him, he could not remember where he'd left Rutland."

There was silence for a moment. Then Richard prodded Edward again with the toe of his shoe.

"You, sir," he shouted, "will mount up with me and a party of men-at-arms and set out to find Rutland. We'll search until we find him. If I find he's been taken hostage by the other side, you'll pay dearly for this, do you understand?"

Edward went white.

"Good God, man," thundered Richard, "there's a war on. Or were you so sunk in debauchery you forgot that too?"

A day later they returned with Rutland and the lame horse. Edward was given a sound beating by the sergeant-at-arms to curb his tendency to be irresponsible. My lord believed the beating would teach him that lesson.

Chapter 27
Spring to Fall 1459

As the shadows grew shorter and the sun rose higher in the sky during the spring of 1459, York at Ludlow and Salisbury at Middleham, summoned their vast following of tenants and retainers to counter the activities of the queen and her conscripted army. Late in June, the king held a great council at Coventry, attended by the Queen and five-year-old Prince Édouard. All lords were summoned to attend, including York and Salisbury. Instead they sent an urgent message to Warwick at Calais, begging him to come to their aid.

Warwick raised two hundred men-at-arms and four hundred archers, all of whom wore red jackets sporting his badge of the bear and the ragged staff. Leaving Cecylee's brother and his uncle William Neville, Lord Fauconberg, in charge of the Calais garrison, Warwick crossed to England and landed at Sandwich in Kent. Not pausing to draw breath, he pressed onto London.

On September 22, 1459, Warwick entered London unopposed. He left the next day at the head of a well-armed force, making for Warwick Castle where the Yorkist lords had planned to meet. However, the queen's army got to Warwick Castle before Warwick did, and since Warwick did not have enough men to risk a confrontation, he turned his army toward Ludlow where York and his army waited.

Meanwhile, Salisbury left Middleham for Ludlow with his army. On September 23, Salisbury was approaching Market Drayton when his scouts warned him the route was blocked by part of the queen's army. He drew up his forces in battle order on nearby Blore Heath and waited.

By dark, the Yorkists were victorious, and Salisbury anxiously pressed on to the safety of Ludlow. Unfortunately, the queen was waiting with the rest of her army at Eccleshall Castle, not ten miles away. His solution was subterfuge:

Salisbury gave his cannon to an Augustinian friar with instructions to fire it off intermittently during the night.

When my lady queen arrived the next morning, she found a frightened friar, a deserted campsite, and a field strewn with corpses. Salisbury was nowhere to be seen for he had already arrived at Ludlow.

Chapter 28
October 1459

Queen Marguerite wasted no time. She mustered an army of thirty thousand and marched towards Ludlow. Richard responded by leading an army of twenty-five thousand out of Ludlow toward Worcester with the aim of getting to London. The queen's army blocked him, however, so he returned to Ludlow, encamping south of town at Ludford Bridge.

On the evening of the tenth day of October, the queen arrived in Ludlow and pitched tents.

A murmuring of male voices came from the direction of the great hall. It was late, pitch black and cold. Cecylee lit a lantern, slipped out of bed, put on a fur-lined robe and slippers, and went to investigate.

"Aren't you going to fight a battle?" she said as she entered.

Richard came and took her hands.

"Our men are deserting. They are going over to the other side as we speak."

She shivered. "What will you do?"

"We are going abroad, for we must escape capture," said Salisbury.

"My lord father and I are going to Calais to bide our time," said Warwick. "We will return to fight when the time is ripe."

"We'll go to Ireland," said Richard, putting a hand on Rutland's shoulder.

"I shall stay," said Edward, "and take my lady mother, my brothers, and my sister Margaret to the abbey at Wigmore."

"No," said Cecylee.

"Cis! It's for your own good!" exclaimed Richard.

"There is no time to get us to safety," she replied. "Besides, the country is crawling with Lancastrian spies."

"Mother," protested Edward. "You are not safe here."

"I shall stay and intercede for the people of Ludlow," she remarked, lifting her chin.

Five pairs of male eyes stared at her, widening in disbelief.

Richard interposed. "I'll not allow it," he said, his mouth tightening into a grim line.

"They'll not harm a woman with three children. We shall dress in our finest clothes and array ourselves in front of the market cross in Ludlow. We'll be on public view. They'll not dare to mistreat us."

The silence was broken by Salisbury's sudden bark of laughter. "How like Mama you look. Do you remember the night when she expected a Percy raid and had you spirited off to the South of England under armed escort?"

Cecylee smiled at the memory. Mama had acted like a tigress to save her.

"What of Margaret?" asked Rutland quietly.

As usual, he'd found the weak point in the plan. Cecylee was not happy at the thought of her beautiful thirteen-year-old daughter being surrounded by rude soldiers.

"I'll not allow it," repeated Richard.

"We have no choice," she replied. "It is imperative that you all leave, and leave now. There is not a moment to lose."

The silence held, and then York nodded somberly.

Salisbury, Edward, and Warwick said their farewells quickly and left. Richard wrapped his arms around her and gave her a peck on the cheek.

"I leave Ludlow in your care."

He signaled to Rutland, who knelt at Cecylee's feet for her blessing.

Then, they were gone.

About the Author

Cynthia Sally Haggard was born and raised in Surrey, England. About thirty years ago she came to the United States and has lived there ever since in the Mid-Atlantic region. She has had four careers, violinist, cognitive scientist, medical writer and novelist. Yes, she is related to H. Rider Haggard, the author of SHE and KING SOLOMONS'S MINES. (He was a younger brother of her great-grandfather.) She got into novel writing by accident, when an instructor announced one day that each member of his class had to produce five pages of their next novel. She took a deep breath and began. She hasn't stopped since.

Connect with me online at my blog: http://spunstories.com/

Author's Note

Thwarted Queen is set in the hundred years that led up to the Reformation in England. During Cecylee's lifetime from 1415 to 1495, the church in England was ruled by the Pope in Rome, as it had been for nearly one thousand years. The Wars of the Roses were therefore not about religion, for everyone worshipped in the same way.

Thwarted Queen naturally divides into four books. *Book One: The Bride Price* is about Cecylee's girlhood. *Book Two: One Seed Sown* is about her love-affair with Blaybourne. *Book Three: The Gilded Cage* is about Richard of York's political career from 1445 to his death in 1460, and covers the opening of the Wars of the Roses. *Book Four: Two Murders Reaped* is about Cecylee's actions in old age, and how she may have had a hand in the murder of the two little princes in the Tower. I used different points of view to convey mood and setting. *The Bride Price* is written in first-person present to capture the freshness of a young girl's voice. *One Seed Sown* is written in first-person past to make Cecylee seem older and more mature. *The Gilded Cage* had to be written in third-person to capture all of the different voices and the complexity of Richard's political life. *Two Murders Reaped* is written in first person past, to capture the voice of the old woman that Cecylee became.

In thinking about Cecylee and what kind of person she must have been to have lead the kind of life you have just read about, I decided I needed a heroine. I needed someone that Cecylee could emulate both as an impressionable young girl and as an older woman. I chose Queen Alainor of Aquitaine, known as Eleanor of Aquitaine to modern readers. She was a real person who lived between 1120 and 1204. Like Cecylee, she lived to a great age and was the mother of two Kings of England; Richard I *Coeur de Lion* (*the Lionheart*), who reigned from 1189 to 1199, and King John, who reigned from 1199 to 1216. She repeatedly broke the rules of what was considered seemly behavior for ladies. Her first act of independence came when she divorced her first husband – Louis VII of France – and married Henry Plantagenet, who became Henry II of England. Later on, after she inspired her sons to rebel against her husband, he locked her up for sixteen years. However, she outlived him, and was let out of prison by her son Richard I. She ruled England for King Richard during his many absences, and won a reputation for fair dealing and wise judgement at the many assizes she held throughout the country. I saw in her the perfect role model for the young and subversive Cecylee.

Why didn't I choose Joan of Arc to be Cecylee's heroine? Because she didn't make her appearance until 1429, and the story of Cecylee's girlhood in *Thwarted Queen* covers the years 1424-1425.

The most controversial part of Cecylee's early life is her betrothal in October 1424. Most historians think she married Richard at that point, and the young couple went to live at the court of King Henry VI. Though this is certainly possible, I made the ceremony a betrothal because I found it hard to believe that Cecylee didn't produce any children for fourteen years. Cecylee was fecund, her children were born in 1438, 1439, 1441, 1442, 1443, 1444, 1446, 1447, 1448,

1449, 1450, 1452 and 1455. Although she was only nine years old in 1424, she could have started producing children by 1430, when she was fourteen turning fifteen. I reasoned that she was not living with Richard until 1437 at the earliest, and that the reason she wasn't living with Richard was because she wasn't married to him.

In thinking about who might have stopped the marriage, I noticed that her father died in 1425 when she was ten years old, and that Richard's wardship passed into her mother's hands. The person most likely to have prevented this marriage was Cecylee's mother Countess Joan. The reason for doing so probably stemmed from the fact that Cecylee was the youngest daughter and all of Countess Joan's other daughters had already been married off and left the family. It is also possible that Countess Joan did not like Richard. I used a fictional episode toward the end of *Book One: The Bride Price* to motivate her dislike.

It seems that Countess Joan was interested in literature. She may have leant two books to King Henry V (her half-grand-nephew) when he went to fight the French at the Battle of Agincourt. And Hoccleve may have dedicated one of his books to her. It is true that Geoffrey Chaucer was Countess Joan's uncle-by-marriage and so she probably owned some of the original manuscripts, which have since disappeared. I do not know if Countess Joan held a reading circle, but it would have been typical of the time period for her to do so. I understand that Abbesses would ride from one great house to another with provocative manuscripts tucked away in their saddle-bags, using the reading circles as a forum for subversive activity, rather like the women writers of Afghanistan who carried on under the guise of sewing circles, as described in *The Sewing Circles of Herat*. (Anyone who has read the *Wife of Bath's Tale* knows how subversive it is.) Apart from the *Wife of Bath*, I have also included some lines from Chaucer's *Parliament of Fowls* and the opening of *The Owl and the Nightingale* – which was written anonymously in around 1272 – to give a flavor of the times and some idea of the kind of literature they were reading. Of course I could not quote Shakespeare, as he was not born until 1564.

The songs were also chosen to be representative of the period. Blaybourne's chanson *Plus Bele que Flor* (More Lovely Than A Flower), and Cecylee's songs *I Cannot Help It If I Rarely Sing* and *This Lovely Star Of The Sea* come from the Montpellier Codex of the 13th century. It is quite possible that people continued to sing these songs well into the 15th century, making changes as they went along.

You may wonder why I chose to believe the tale of Cecylee's affair with an archer on the Rouen garrison. After all, Anne Easter Smith, who has written her own novel about Cecylee, dismisses it out of hand. I believed it both because it had a ring of truth to it, and because it explains so many things. It explains, for example, why Cecylee helped to nullify Edward IV's will shortly after his death, and why Richard III repeatedly sought his mother's counsel and seemed to have had a much closer relationship with her than Edward IV ever did. It also explains Richard of York's actions, why he had a sumptuous christening ceremony for his second surviving son Rutland, but not for Edward. And why he chose to exile himself to Ireland with Rutland, but not Edward. During that moment of crisis in 1459 when everything seemed lost, it is interesting that Edward sat it out in Calais with his mother's relatives, rather than being by Richard of York's side.

Of course, Cecylee's lover Blaybourne presented his own set of problems. Scarcely anything is known about him, except that he was an archer on the Rouen garrison during the summer of 1441 when Cecylee's husband Richard was away campaigning against the French in Pontoise. I was forced to make up everything about his life and circumstances and I tried to draw a character who was plausible for the fifteenth century, making him someone who would have gotten his opportunities in life from his education in a monastery.

To give a cultural read on the risks that Cecylee was taking, I included two stories about jealous husbands and the ways in which they punished their wives. Black Fulk, more commonly known in Anjou as *Foulques Nerra*, was Count of Anjou from 987, when he was around fifteen years old, until his death in 1040. He had a violent temperament, so the story that he burned his first wife Helizabeth in the market square at Angers after discovering her in bed with a lover, may well be true.

When twenty-one-year-old Parisina (or Laura) Malatesta was discovered in bed with her twenty-year-old stepson Ugo d'Este, her husband (and his father) Niccolo III d'Este ordered their executions. They were beheaded on May 21, 1425, when Cecylee had just turned ten.

Beginning with *Book Three: The Gilded Cage*, the novel becomes much more factually-based as Cecylee emerges from the shadows. I followed the opinions of historians Alison Weir and Michael K. Jones in trying to reconstruct this period, especially Alison Weir's *The Wars of the Roses* and *The Princes in the Tower*, and Michael K. Jones' *Bosworth 1485: The Psychology of Battle*.

It is true that Cecylee's six-year-old daughter was married off in 1446. I do not know if this was Richard's way of punishing his wife for taking a lover, but Nan was forced to marry someone who was notorious for his cruelty. If you are one of those readers wondering why a six-year-old bride would be more useful than an older girl - given that she would not be able to bear children for several years - you have to remember that these girls were used as pawns in huge land transfers. The reason for marrying a young child now rather than later was because the family she was marrying into was impatient to acquire the wealth of the land that she brought as a dowry.

Obviously, there must have been a huge problem of child abuse, for these young girls were taken from their families, and sent off to live with their in-laws at the time of marriage. Legally, the husband became the child-bride's liege lord, which meant that he had total control over her. The child-bride was thrust upon the mercy of her husband and in-laws, in a situation that is not unlike the one that occurs in India today. This practice was not uncommon six hundred years ago. In *Thwarted Queen* there are at least two other examples; Cecylee's sister Alainor, who was forced into a marriage when she was five years old. When her 18-year-old bridegroom died, she was married to the Earl of Northumberland's heir when she was seven. The other example is Richard's sister Isabel who was married when she was about four years old to Sir Thomas Grey. That marriage was annulled for reasons that are not clear; but it is possible that Isabel was badly treated. By contrast, if the young girl was betrothed, she continued to be under the jurisdiction of her parents and lived with her family of origin until the marriage took place.

It is not known what happened to the little princes in the Tower (the sons and heirs of Edward IV). In trying to reconstruct what happened I have followed the ideas of Alison Weir in her *The Princes in the Tower*. However, not all historians agree that Richard III murdered his nephews, so I have given an alternative explanation at the end of the novel, in which I suggest that the younger brother, Richard, Duke of York, was smuggled out of the country and lived in Burgundy. If you are wondering why everyone is so certain that the elder brother, Edward V died in the Tower, it is because there are records showing that the poor young man was suffering from a severe ear infection in the summer of 1483. Without modern medicine, it is almost certain that his condition would have killed him within the year.

A couple of incidents in *Thwarted Queen* are based on the testimony of people alive at the time. Cecylee's tirade against Edward IV – in which she publicly announces he is illegitimate – is based on what Dominic Mancini, an Italian diplomat of the time, wrote. I have followed the historian Michael K. Jones' opinion that Cecylee was exiled to Berkhamsted Castle in March of 1469, and thus Cecylee's explosion occurred shortly beforehand. Echoes of this can be seen in Shakespeare's *Richard III*, except that in the play Cecylee's tirade is directed against Richard III. Shakespeare's play can be treated as propaganda on behalf of the Tudors. He did everything he could to blacken the character of

Richard III, and so one can almost treat the play as a mirror-image of what actually occurred.

The other incident is Edward's marriage to Lady Eleanor Butler. This is based upon the testimony of Robert Stillington, Bishop of Bath and Wells. It is not known when the marriage actually took place, but I have set it in April 1462, because it gave a plausible time-frame for Lady Eleanor to have had a child before Edward met Elisabeth Woodville, whom he married two years later in May 1464. As in the novel, these facts did not come to light until after Edward's death. People at the time had difficulty believing this story because it was so obviously in Richard of Gloucester's interests to claim that Edward's marriage to Elisabeth Woodville was bigamous. However, the story had the ring of plausibility for me, because Edward was a notorious womanizer who may have been attracted to older widows. (Both Elisabeth Woodville and Eleanor Talbot were Lancastrian widows. Elisabeth Woodville was five years older than Edward, and Eleanor Butler would have been about seven years older.)

As far as I know, there is no evidence that Cecylee ever referred to her daughter-in-law as *The Serpent*, though it is true that she was dismayed by Edward's marriage and the two ladies seemed not to have liked each other. I picked that particular nickname because I felt it conveyed volumes about how Cecylee felt about Edward's Queen. Élisabeth's name for Cecylee, *good mother*, is meant to sound disrespectful. It is meant to sound like *Goodwife*, which although it was a polite form of address for women, only applied to those of the lowest social classes. By calling Cecylee *good mother*, rather than *Madam*, Élisabeth conveyed her animosity towards her mother-in-law. The encounters between Cecylee and Queen Élisabeth are fictional, but are based on fact, such as the Queen's rapacious relatives wiping the aristocratic marriage market clean and Cecylee's resulting problems in trying to find suitable marriage partners for her children. Cecylee did style herself *Queen By Right* and she did move into the Queen's apartments, forcing her son Edward to build a separate wing for his new wife. The speech in which she tells Edward off about his marriage is based upon Sir Thomas More's account as reported by Michael K. Jones.

Writing about the past forces historical novelists to confront the fraught issue of dates of birth. It is often difficult to pin an age on a person, especially minor female characters, because dates of birth were not systematically recorded. The reader should therefore take the ages of most of the characters as approximations.

Documents from the time provided a fascinating glimpse of Cecylee's life in her later years. *Orders and Rules of the Princess Cecill* and *The Rules of the House* show a strong-minded yet kind woman running a tight ship at Berkhamsted Castle. I hope you enjoyed the quotations from these sources. In her will of 1495, Cecylee makes reference to two nearby convents:

> *"Also I geve to the house of Assherugge a chesibule and 2 tunicles of crymsyn damaske embrawdered with thre albes. Also I geve to the house of Saint Margaretes twoo auter clothes with a crucifix and a vestiment of grene vellet..."*

I haven't been able to trace a convent of Saint Margaret, but there was a convent at Ashridge, about four miles from Berkhamsted castle, and so I chose to place Cecylee's friends from her later years there. (In the fifteenth century, most people didn't think twice about walking four miles).

Such documents also give us clues to how things were pronounced. In Cecylee's will of 1495, for example, she refers to Fotheringhay as "Fodringhey", so I used that pronunciation in the scene where Richard talks about his favorite residence to Queen Marguerite d'Anjou.

Lastly, readers may wonder how I came to choose the name *Cecylee*. Not wanting to get caught up in the Cecily/ Cicely controversy, I thought it would be interesting to see how Cecylee herself spelt her name. Her will is in the public domain, and it seems that she signed it *Cecylee*. However, her handwriting is extremely difficult to read – it looks like the signature of someone who does not write much – so it is possible that she actually spelled her name *Cecylle*. In the fifteenth century spelling varied widely and great ladies like Cecylee usually dictated their letters and papers to scribes who came from different regions of the country and spelled things differently. According to the Richard III society, Cecylee in her lifetime was addressed as *Cecill, Cecille, Cecyll* but the most usual form of the name was *Cecylee*. And so I went with that version of the name, knowing that it would be easy for English-speaking readers to figure out how to pronounce it. (It is pronounced in the exact same way as the more modern spelling of the name, *Cecily*.) If I had been writing for French readers, I probably would have called her *Cecylle*, because that is closer to the French version of the name *Cécile*.

It was an honor as well as great fun to have Cecylee materialize from the fifteenth century and talk to me about her life. I hope you enjoyed reading this novel as much as I enjoyed writing it.

Cynthia Sally Haggard
Washington D. C., 2011.

Below is a selection of sources I used in researching *Thwarted Queen*, followed by a list of characters in the novel.

Books

Amt, Emilie (1992). *Women's Lives in Medieval Europe: A Sourcebook.*

Ankarloo, Bengt and Stuart Clark (2002). *Witchcraft and Magic in Europe. Volume 3: The Middle Ages.*

Anonymous 4. *Love's Illusion: Music from the Montpellier Codex, 13th century.*

Baldwin, David (2004). *Elizabeth Woodville: Mother of the Princes in the Tower.*

Cartidge, Neil (2001). *The Owl and the Nightingale: Text and Translation*. University of Exeter Press.

Chaucer, Geoffrey (1382/2004). *The Parliament of Birds*. Hesperus Press.

Chantilly, Musée Condé, Jean Longnon, Raymond Cazelles (1489/1989). *The Très Riches Heures of Jean, Duc de Berry*.

Cobb, John Wolstenholme (1883/2008). History & Antiquities of Berkhamsted.

Gies, Frances (1991). *Life in a Medieval Village*

Gies, Frances (1998). *A Medieval Family: The Pastons of Fifteenth-Century England*.

Hardy, Robert (1992). *Longbow: A Social and Military History*.

Houston, Mary G. (1996). *Medieval Costume in England and France: The 13th, 14th and 15th centuries*.

Jones, Michael K. (2003). *Bosworth 1485: The Psychology of a Battle* (Revealing History Series).

Landsberg, Sylvia (2003). *The Medieval Garden*.

Parlett, David (1991). *A History of Card Games*.

Ross, Charles (1998). *Edward IV* (The English Monarchs Series).

Smith, A. H. (1978). *Three Northumbrian Poems*. (Exeter Medieval Texts and Studies).
     Exeter University Press.

Weir, Alison (1995). *The Princes in the Tower*.

Weir, Alison (1996). *The Wars of the Roses.*

Weir, Alison (2009). *Mistress of the Monarchy: The Life of Katherine Swynford, Duchess of Lancaster.*

Whiteman, Robin and Rob Talbot Brother (1996). *Brother Cadfael's Herb Garden: An Illustrated Companion to Medieval Plants and Their Uses.*

Characters

(in order of appearance)

WILLIAM DE LA POLE, 4th EARL OF SUFFOLK
(1396-1450). DUKE OF SUFFOLK from 1448.
Succeeded Cardinal Beaufort as head of the Court Party.
Friend of Queen Marguerite. Murdered May 2, 1450 on
the gunwales of a boat, on his way to France.

MARGUERITE D'ANJOU (1429-1482), daughter of Réné
of Anjou and Ysabeau of Lorraine. Married King Henry
VI of England in 1445.

HENRY VI, KING OF ENGLAND, DUKE OF
LANCASTER (1421-1471), son of Henry V and Catrine
de Valois, he ruled England from 1437. His rule was a
disaster in every conceivable way, because he was a weak
king, who was easily led.

HENRY, CARDINAL BEAUFORT (born circa 1381, died
1447), brother to Countess Joan, younger son of John of
Gaunt and Catrine de Roet. Head of the Court Party until
his death.

HENRY V, KING OF ENGLAND (1387-1422). Victor at
Agincourt in 1415, he was a strong leader who died
suddenly of dysentery. Father of Henry VI.

YSABEAU, DUCHESS OF LORRAINE (born circa 1400,
died 1453), was the eldest daughter and heiress of Charles
II, Duke of Lorraine. She married Réné d'Anjou in 1419.
Marguerite d'Anjou, Queen of England was her youngest
child.

RÉNÉ, DUKE OF ANJOU (1409-1480), son of Louis II
d'Anjou and Yolande of Aragon, he was the brother of
Marie d'Anjou, Queen of France, brother-in-law to King
Charles VII of France, and father of Marguerite d'Anjou,
Queen of England.

PHILIP III DUKE OF BURGUNDY "THE
GOOD" (1396-1467). A staunch friend to the House of
York.

YOLANDE, DUCHESS OF ARAGON (1384-1442), Marguerite's grandmother, and *de facto* ruler of France from 1417 until her death.

JOAN OF ARC (born circa 1412, died 1431) was the charismatic French heroine who rallied the French to fight the English and succeeded in getting the dauphin crowned King Charles VII of France. The English tried her for heresy and burned her at stake in the marketplace of Rouen on May 30, 1431.

HUMPHREY PLANTAGENET, DUKE OF GLOUCESTER (1390-1447), younger brother to King Henry V. Married (a) Jacqueline, Countess of Hainault and Holland, (b) Eleanor Cobham, his mistress. Negotiated marriage between Richard and Cecylee. Beloved mentor and friend to Richard of York. Head of the opposition to the Court Party.

CHARLES, COUNT OF NEVERS (1414-1464). A suitor to Marguerite d'Anjou, Charles was accused of practicing sorcery so that he could supplant Philip of Burgundy's son as heir. He fled to France and died soon after.

CECYLEE NEVILLE, DUCHESS OF YORK (1415-1495).

LADY JOAN PLANTAGENET (born circa 1438, died circa 1441).

RICHARD PLANTAGENET, "DICKON" (1411-1460), 3RD DUKE OF YORK from 1415, EARL OF MARCH from 1425, EARL OF CAMBRIDGE and EARL OF ULSTER from 1432. Cecylee's husband, they married circa 1437.

EDWARD, EARL OF MARCH (1442-1483), Cecylee's illegitimate son with Blaybourne.

EDMUND PLANTAGENET, EARL OF RUTLAND (1443-1460), Cecylee and Richard's eldest surviving son. Richard treated this son as his heir.

ROLLO, DUKE OF NORMANDY (born circa 846, died circa 931) was baptized in 912. A Viking leader, the fiefdom of Normandy was created for him by King Charles III of France in 911. In return for this territory, Rollo and his warriors were to protect the northern

French coast from Viking raids and convert to
Christianity. He became the great-great-great-grandfather
of William the Conqueror.

WILLIAM, "THE BASTARD" (born circa 1028, died 1087)
DUKE OF NORMANDY from 1035, KING WILLIAM
I OF ENGLAND "THE CONQUEROR" from 1066.
William was the illegitimate son of Robert I, Duke of
Normandy, and Herleva "The Maid of Falaise". As the
only son of Duke Robert, he was named his heir soon
after his birth, and succeeded him as Duke of Normandy
in 1035, when he was around 7 years old. He is famous
for winning the Battle of Hastings in 1066, which
brought Norman rule to England.

LADY ELIZABETH PLANTAGENET "BETH" (born
1444, died circa 1504), second surviving daughter of
Cecylee and Richard, married to John de la Pole, Duke of
Suffolk in 1458.

LADY ANNE PLANTAGENET, "NAN" (1439-1476),
eldest surviving daughter of Cecylee and Richard, married
to Henry Holland, Duke of Exeter in 1447.

MARIE D'ANJOU, QUEEN OF FRANCE (1404-1463),
eldest daughter of Louis II of Anjou and Yolande of
Aragon, she married Charles VII of France in 1422. She
was aunt to Marguerite d'Anjou, Queen of England.

CHARLES DE VALOIS, DUKE D'ORLÉANS (1394-1465.
He was captured by the English in 1415 after the victory
at Agincourt, and remained a prisoner for 24 years, during
which time he wrote over 500 poems. He must have been
charming, for his English captors became his best friends.

JACQUETTA DE ST POL, DUCHESS OF BEDFORD
(born circa 1416, died 1472). Also known as
JACQUETTA OF LUXEMBOURG, she was the eldest
daughter of Peter I, Count of St Pol and Margherita del
Balzo of Andria. Married (a) John, Duke of Bedford
(1389-1435) younger brother to King Henry V, (b) Sir
Richard Woodville (1405-1469). Mother to Élisabeth
Woodville, Queen of England.

SIR RICHARD WOODVILLE (1405-1469). EARL RIVERS from 1448. He was the son of Richard Woodville, a squire from Maidstone, Kent, and father to Élisabeth Woodville, Queen of England. The name is also spelt "Wydeville".

ÉLISABETH WOODVILLE (born circa 1437, died 1492). Married (a) Sir John Grey of Groby (born circa 1432, died 1461), (b) Edward IV of England (1442-1483).

ELEANOR BEAUCHAMP, DUCHESS OF SOMERSET (1407-1467), second daughter of Richard de Beauchamp, 13th Earl of Warwick and Elizabeth de Berkeley. She was the wife of Edmund Beaufort 2nd Duke of Somerset, and a great friend to Queen Marguerite, and sister to Margaret Talbot and Lisette Latimer.

CHARLES, COUNT OF MAINE (1414-1472) was the third son of Louis II of Anjou and Yolande of Aragon. He was uncle to Marguerite d'Anjou, Queen of England.

ALICE CHAUCER, COUNTESS OF SUFFOLK (1404-1475). Daughter of Thomas Chaucer and Matilda Burghersh, she was a granddaughter of Geoffrey Chaucer the poet. In 1430, she married William de la Pole, Earl of Suffolk.

CATRINE DE VALOIS (1401-1437), daughter of Charles VI of France and Isabelle of Bavaria (the patroness of Christine de Pizan), Catrine married Henry V of England in 1420 as part of the peace settlement after Agincourt. She had one child with Henry V, a son who became Henry VI of England. After Henry V's death in 1422, she had a relationship with Owen ap Maredudd ap Tudor, (known as Owen Tudor in England) and produced five children, including Edmund Tudor, Earl of Richmond and Jasper Tudor, Earl of Pembroke. The Tudor Dynasty descends from Edmund Tudor.

GEOFFREY CHAUCER (born circa 1340, died between 1400 and 1402). Married Philippa de Roet, sister to Catrine de Roet (Lady Katherine Swynford), Cecylee's grandmother. He was therefore granduncle-by-marriage to Cecylee. The greatest poet of his day, his is most famous for THE CANTERBURY TALES. In his day, he was also famous for THE PARLIAMENT OF THE FOWLS, and THE BOOK OF THE DUCHESS, written circa 1469 to commemorate the death of his patron's wife Blanche of Lancaster from the plague.

ELEANOR COBHAM (born circa 1400, died between 1452 and 1454). She was the daughter of Reginald Cobham, 3rd Lord Cobham, and his first wife, Eleanor Culpeper. She was the mistress, then second wife of Humphrey, Duke of Gloucester. In 1441, she was convicted of trying to kill Henry VI by means of witchcraft, and imprisoned for the rest of her life.

LEONARDO BRUNI "ARETINO" (born circa 1370, died 1444), was an Italian humanist who has been called the first modern historian.

TIBERIUS (42 BCE to 37 CE), he was Roman Emperor from 14 CE. His reign began well but ended in terror.

CALIGULA (12 CE to 41 CE), he was Roman Emperor from 37 CE. He is famous for his cruelty, extravagance, and sexual perversity.

CLAUDIUS (10 BCE to 54 CE), he was Roman Emperor from 41 CE. Claudius was constantly forced to shore up his position, and this resulted in the deaths of many Roman senators.

NERO (37 CE to 68 CE), he was Roman Emperor from 54 CE. Nero's rule is often associated with tyranny and extravagance.

ADAM MOLEYNS, BISHOP OF CHICHESTER (died 1450), he was an active supporter of William de la Pole, 4th Earl of Suffolk.

JOHN DE MOWBRAY, 3RD DUKE OF NORFOLK (1415-1461). Son of John de Mowbray, 2nd Duke of Norfolk and Lady Catrine de Neville. One of Cecylee's nephews, he was the premier peer of the realm. He switched sides many times during the Wars of the Roses, but his intervention in the Battle of Towton was decisive in winning it for Edward IV.

EDMUND MORTIMER, 5TH EARL OF MARCH
(1391-1425), he was a son of Roger Mortimer and
Alianore de Holland. His elder sister Anne married
Richard, Earl of Cambridge, and became the mother of
Richard, Duke of York. He was therefore uncle to
Cecylee's husband. He died without heirs, so Richard
inherited his title.

CHARLES VII, KING OF FRANCE (1403-1461), he is the
King of France who was famously crowned by Joan of
Arc.

RICHARD DE BEAUCHAMP, 13TH EARL OF
WARWICK (1382-1439), was the son of Thomas de
Beauchamp, 12th Earl of Warwick and Margaret Ferrers.
By the terms of Henry V's will, he was made guardian to
the infant King Henry VI. He married Elizabeth de
Berkeley, with whom he had three daughters: Margaret,
Countess of Shrewsbury (Cecylee's dearest friend),
Eleanor, Countess of Somerset (a great friend to Queen
Marguerite d'Anjou) and Elizabeth, Lady Latimer
"Lisette" (one of Cecylee's worst enemies). By his second
wife Isabel le Despencer, he had two children, Henry,
who succeeded him as 14th Earl, and Anne, 16th
Countess of Warwick who was married to Richard
Neville, son and heir of Richard Neville, 5th Earl of
Salisbury.

EDMUND BEAUFORT, 4TH EARL OF SOMERSET,
2ND DUKE OF SOMERSET (1406-1455), fourth son
of John Beaufort, 1st Earl of Somerset and Margaret
Holland, he was a nephew to Countess Joan. Succeeded
Suffolk as head of the Court Party. Possible lover to
Queen Marguerite, and father of her son Édouard. Killed
at the first Battle of St. Albans.

MADELEINE DE VALOIS (1443-1495), daughter of
Charles VII of France. She was proposed as a possible
wife to Cecylee's illegitimate son, Edward, Earl of March,
later King Edward IV.

ANNE DE CAUX "ANNETTE" (dates unknown),
nursemaid and governess to Cecylee's children.

EDMUND OF LANGLEY, 1ST DUKE OF YORK
(1341-1402), was the fourth surviving son of King
Edward III, after Edward the Black Prince, Lionel of
Antwerp and John of Gaunt. He married Isabella of
Castile and produced two sons and a daughter: Edward of
Norwich, Richard of Conisburgh and Constance of York.

EDWARD OF NORWICH, EARL OF RUTLAND
(1373-1415), 2ND DUKE OF YORK from 1402. He was
the son and heir of Edmund of Langley, 1st Duke of
York. He married Philippa de Mohun, a widow, but had
no children. He was killed at the Battle of Agincourt.

RICHARD OF CONISBURGH, EARL OF CAMBRIDGE
(1375-1415). The second son of Edmund of Langley, he
married Lady Anne de Mortimer, a descendant of
Edward III via his second son Lionel of Antwerp. They
had two children: Lady Isabel Plantagenet and Richard,
Duke of York. He would have been Cecylee's father-in-
law, if he hadn't been executed for treason in 1415.

LADY ELIZABETH BEAUCHAMP "LISETTE" (born
circa 1421, died 1480), youngest daughter of Richard de
Beauchamp, 13th Earl of Warwick and Elizabeth de
Berkeley. She was married to Cecylee's brother George,
Lord Latimer, sister to Margaret Talbot and Eleanor
Beaufort.

ABBOT JOHN WHETHAMSTEAD (died 1465), the Abbot
of the Benedictine Abbey of St. Albans, he was closely
associated with the humanistic work of Humphrey, Duke
of Gloucester.

RICHARD NEVILLE, 5th EARL OF SALISBURY
(1400-1460). Eldest son of Joan de Beaufort and Ralph
Neville, 1st Earl of Westmorland. Earl of Salisbury in
right of his wife, Alice de Montacute, the wealthy heiress
to the Salisbury title and lands.

LADY MARGARET PLANTAGENET (1446-1503),
youngest surviving daughter of Richard and Cecylee, she
married Charles the Bold, Duke of Burgundy in 1468.

JOHN DE LA POLE, 2ND DUKE OF SUFFOLK (born
1442, died circa 1492), son of William de la Pole, was

married to Beth Plantagenet, daughter of Richard and
Cecylee in 1458.

EDMUND TUDOR, EARL OF RICHMOND (1430-1456),
son of Owen Tudor and Catrine de Valois, he was
married to Lady Margaret Beaufort and became the father
of Henry, Earl of Richmond, later Henry VII, King of
England. He died of the plague in 1456.

JASPER TUDOR, EARL OF PEMBROKE (born circa
1431, died 1495), son of Catrine de Valois and Owen
Tudor, younger brother of Edmund Tudor. He was an
adventurer who was loyal to the Lancastrian cause, and
brought up his nephew Henry Tudor, Earl of Richmond.
When Henry Tudor became king, he restored all of his
uncle's lands and titles. In 1485, Jasper was married to
Catherine Woodville, formerly Duchess of Buckingham,
who was a sister to Queen Élisabeth Woodville.

JOHN HOLLAND, 2ND DUKE OF EXETER
(1385-1447), the second son of John Holland 1st Duke of
Exeter, and Elizabeth of Lancaster, whose father was
John of Gaunt, Duke of Lancaster. In 1427, he was
married to Lady Anne Stafford and became the father of
Henry Holland, 3rd Duke of Exeter.

HENRY HOLLAND, 3RD DUKE OF EXETER
(1430-1475), son and heir of John Holland, 2nd Duke of
Exeter, was married to Lady Anne Plantagenet, eldest
daughter of Richard and Cecylee in 1447. So cruel was he
that during his tenure as Constable of the Tower of
London, the rack became known as "the Duke of
Exeter's daughter."

ANNE STAFFORD, DUCHESS OF EXETER (died 1432),
the first wife of John Holland, 2nd Duke of Exeter, she
was the mother of Henry Holland, 3rd Duke of Exeter.

BEATRIX OF PORTUGAL, DUCHESS OF EXETER
(1386-1439) was the illegitimate daughter of John I of
Portugal and Ines Pires. In 1432, she married John
Holland, 2nd Duke of Exeter and became his second
wife. She died in Bordeaux in 1439.

LORD WILLIAM PLANTAGENET (born 1447, died as a child), Cecylee and Richard's third son.

LORD JOHN PLANTAGENET (born 1448, died as a child), Cecylee' and Richard's fourth son.

LORD GEORGE PLANTAGENET (1449-1478), Cecylee and Richard's fifth son, he was DUKE OF CLARENCE from 1461. In 1469, he married his cousin Lady Isabel Neville, daughter and heiress to Richard Neville, 16th Earl of Warwick, known as "The Kingmaker".

LORD THOMAS PLANTAGENET (born 1450, died as a child), Cecylee and Richard's sixth son.

SIR WILLIAM OLDHALL (born circa 1390, died 1460), Chamberlain to Richard, Duke of York, Speaker of the House of Commons between 1450-1451.

RICHARD OF BORDEAUX (born 1367, died circa 1400) KING RICHARD II OF ENGLAND from 1377. He was the son of Edward, the Black Prince, the eldest son and heir of Edward III. When his grandfather died in 1377, he became King of England at the age of 10. He was murdered in 1399 on the orders of his cousin Henry of Bolingbroke, probably by starvation.

WILLIAM II, KING OF ENGLAND (born circa 1056, died 1100), he was the third son of William the Conqueror and Matilda of Flanders. On his father's death in 1087, he became King of England. (His elder brother Robert, became Duke of Normandy).

RICHARD NEVILLE 16TH EARL OF WARWICK (1428-1471), eldest son and heir of Richard Neville, 5th Earl of Salisbury and Alice de Montacute, he was one of Cecylee's nephews. He was married to Anne Beauchamp, 16th Countess of Warwick, becoming the 16th Earl in right of his wife.

THOMAS BOURCHIER, BISHOP OF ELY, (born circa 1404, died 1486), ARCHBISHOP OF CANTERBURY from 1454. Younger brother of Henry, Viscount Bourchier, brother-in-law to Richard, Duke of York.

WILLIAM WAYNEFLETE, BISHOP OF WINCHESTER (born circa 1398, died 1486).

LORD RICHARD PLANTAGENET (1452-1485), DUKE
OF GLOUCESTER from 1461, he was Cecylee and
Richard's youngest surviving child. Growing up during
the Wars of the Roses, he was ten years younger than his
half-brother Edward IV.

JOHN TALBOT, 1ST EARL OF SHREWSBURY
(1390-1453). He is remembered for his dashing bravery in
trying to snatch back the territories around Bordeaux for
the English. His murder by the French at Castillon is
thought, by some historians, to have precipitated Henry
VI's 16-month bout of madness, which modern doctors
think was probably catatonic schizophrenia.

ÉDOUARD OF WESTMINSTER, PRINCE OF WALES
(1453-1471), son to Marguerite d'Anjou, and possibly
Henry VI of England or Edmund Beaufort, 1st Duke of
Somerset. Also known as "Edward of Lancaster."

EDWARD THE CONFESSOR (born circa 1003, died 1066),
King of England from 1042 was one of the last Anglo-
Saxon kings of England. Traditionally seen as unworldly
and pious, Edward was canonized in 1161 by Pope
Alexander III. He was Henry VI's favorite saint.

JOHN KEMPE, (died 1454), ARCHBISHOP OF
CANTERBURY from 1452.

ANNE NEVILLE, DUCHESS OF BUCKINGHAM (born
circa 1411, died 1480), Cecylee's sister, she married
Humphrey Stafford, 1st Duke of Buckingham.

ANNE BEAUCHAMP, 16th COUNTESS OF WARWICK
(1426-1492), daughter of Richard de Beauchamp, 13th
Earl of Warwick and Isabel le Despencer, she was
married to Richard Neville, son and heir of Richard
Neville, 5th Earl of Salisbury. The marriage made him the
16th Earl.

SIR JOHN GREY OF GROBY (born circa 1432, died 1461)
was the son and heir of Elizabeth Ferrers, 6th Baroness
Ferrers of Groby and Sir Edward Grey. He was married
to Élisabeth Woodville circa 1452 and they had two
children: Thomas Grey, who later became Marquess of

Dorset, and Sir Richard Grey. Sir John was killed at the Second Battle of St. Albans in 1461.

HENRY BOURCHIER, 2ND COUNT OF EU, 5TH BARON BOURCHIER (1406-1483) 1ST VISCOUNT BOURCHIER from 1446, 1ST EARL OF ESSEX from 1461. In 1426, he married Isabel Plantagenet, Richard's sister, and they had at least eleven children.

HUMPHREY STAFFORD, 6TH EARL OF STAFFORD (1402-1460), 1ST DUKE OF BUCKINGHAM from 1444, he was married to Anne Neville, Cecylee's sister.

HUMPHREY STAFFORD (born circa 1424, died 1458), son of Humphrey Stafford, 1st Duke of Buckingham and Anne Neville, nephew to Cecylee.

HENRY STAFFORD, 2ND DUKE OF BUCKINGHAM (1455-1483), grandson to Anne Neville, and great-nephew to Cecylee. He became Duke of Buckingham on the death of his grandfather.

HENRY PERCY, 2ND EARL OF NORTHUMBERLAND (born circa 1392, died 1455), married to Alainor de Neville, Cecylee's sister. Killed at the First Battle of St. Albans in 1455.

HENRY PERCY, 3RD EARL OF NORTHUMBERLAND, (1421-1461), son of Henry Percy, 2nd Earl of Northumberland and Alainor de Neville, nephew to Cecylee.

JAMES BUTLER, 5TH EARL OF ORMOND (1420-1461), 1ST EARL OF WILTSHIRE from 1449. The earldom of Wiltshire was created for him by Henry VI, but he also served as Lord Treasurer of England during Richard's regency in 1454. However, when the Wars of the Roses broke out in 1455, he fought on the Lancastrian side. He was beheaded at Newcastle in May 1461, by Edward IV, after the Battle of Towton.

LADY URSULA PLANTAGENET (born 1455, died as a baby), Cecylee and Richard's youngest child.

WILLIAM NEVILLE, LORD FAUCONBERG (circa 1409-1463), 1ST EARL OF KENT from 1461, was one of Cecylee's brothers. He was Lord Fauconberg in right of his wife, and some historians think he is an underrated figure in the rise to power of the Yorkists, being a better general than his nephew Warwick "The Kingmaker".

Fictional characters:
CHATELAINE, a cat owned by Cecylee's daughter Nan.
MASTER ELBEUF, Richard's comptroller.
JACINDA, a young girl leaning out of a window, upset at the loss of Anjou pears.
JENET, Cecylee's maid.
PIERRE DE BLAY, *BLAYBOURNE*.
POPELINA, a maid who overhears that the Queen means to seize power for herself.

CPSIA information can be obtained at www.ICGtesting.com
Printed in the USA
BVOW011150010312

284206BV00010B/132/P

9 780984 816927